His Remarkable Bride

By Merry Farmer

HIS REMARKABLE BRIDE

Cover design by Erin Dameron-Hill (the miracle-worker)
Embellishment by © Olgasha I Dreamstime.com

ASIN: B01HH6L4UO
Paperback:
ISBN-13: 9781534857773

ISBN-10: 153485777X

If you'd like to be the first to learn about when the next books in the series come out and more, please sign up for my newsletter here: http://eepurl.com/RQ-KX

Like historical western romance? Come join us in the Pioneer Hearts group on Facebook for games, prizes, exclusive content, and first looks at the latest releases of your favorite historical western authors. https://www.facebook.com/groups/pioneerhearts/

For all those families with tons of kids

The Pellanis, the Echolses, the Coles, the Synnestvedts,
the—

--Wait, why do I know so many families
with eight plus kids?

*All the best
to you, Christine!*

—Mivy Farmer 〔:)〕

Table of Contents

Haskell, Wyoming – 1876

Everybody in Haskell, Wyoming knew that Athos Strong, the town's stationmaster, widower, and father of eight children, needed a new bride. Everybody in Haskell had been encouraging him to petition Charlie Garrett, Virginia Piedmont, and Josephine Evans to send for a mail-order bride for him from Hurst Home—a harbor for women who were endangered or had been ill-used—in Nashville, Tennessee. Everybody clucked and shook their heads behind Athos's back, worrying that his vast brood was getting out of hand without a mother to guide them, and that Athos's sister, Piper, could only do so much to keep the children in line. But it wasn't until after church on a breezy day in April that matters finally came to a head.

It was the first post-church, potluck lunch of the season to be held outside. Everything started out innocently enough. The spring air still had a nip in it, but the sun was out, the grass was beginning to turn green and reach for the sky again, and the men were talking baseball.

"The Haskell Hawks might have won the league last year," Solomon Templesmith, the town's banker, a black man of distinction, and one of the town's wealthiest citizens observed, "But with all the babies you lot are having or are due to have, I can't imagine you'll have the time for adequate practice."

"Not to mention the fact that one of our star outfielders up and moved into town," Mason Montrose, the Hawks' captain, grumbled.

"I'll be playing for the Eastside Eagles this year," Travis confirmed, slapping his brother's back, then shifting to stand next to Solomon. "Although Wendy is due halfway through the season."

Travis grinned from ear to ear as he looked out over the sunny churchyard to his wife, Wendy. Sure enough, Wendy's middle rounded in a good-sized bump. A few months more, and she would bring her and Travis's first child into the world. She wasn't the only one. Wendy stood talking with Corva Haskell, wife of Franklin Haskell, son of the town's founder, cradling her newborn, while Eden Chance was showing off her own brand-new baby. Libby Montrose rounded out the trio of new mothers, though her little girl was a few months older.

Athos Strong grinned along with the rest of the men, but a different kind of emotion rose up through his gut. It was warm and tender, but also hollow and lost. He glanced past the new mothers to his own children. All eight of them were lively and excitable. The younger ones were tearing around the churchyard with their friends— perhaps a little too close to where the adults stood talking or helping themselves to plates of food that had been set out for the potluck. The older ones were in mischievous spirits themselves, by the look of things. Sixteen-year-old Hubert was in a huddle with his buddies, Freddy Chance and Noah Kline, discussing something Noah held, with little Minnie Faraday looking in. Fourteen-year-old twins, Ivy and Heather, were loitering around the church's front stairs with Muriel Chance, Henrietta Plover, and Penny Albee, most likely giggling about boys. Vernon was off in the tall grass with Petey and Matthew Simms. Which left Lael, twins Geneva and Millicent, and four-year-old Thomas, the youngest of the Strong brood, charging through the after-church gathering like a thunderstorm.

"We don't have that problem on the Bonneville Bears." Athos only barely registered Rex Bonneville's comment as he watched the children playing. "I've been strict about letting my men associate with any ladies. Well, other than Bonnie's girls. A man has to have some *female attention*." He smirked at Bonnie Horner, who held his arm with resignation. She gave him a brittle smile in return.

"Your men will play ball again someday," Solomon went on, speaking to Mason. "Take Athos here, for example. His kids are older. He could play easily. Right, Athos? Athos?"

"Hmm?" Athos snapped his thoughts away from his precious, lively, wild children and focused on the conversation.

Solomon, thumped him on the back. "I was saying that you should join the Eastside Eagles this year. We could use your strong arms to replace Charlie's, now that he's retiring."

"You're retiring from baseball?" Athos turned to Charlie Garrett, another of the town's more successful businessman and owner of Hurst Home.

Charlie chuckled. "These old knees have had enough

of running bases. It's time a younger man with muscle replaced me." He nodded to Athos.

Conscious that he looked a bit silly doing it, Athos glanced down at himself. True, working as the stationmaster, loading and unloading crates and shipments and luggage all day, every day had bulked him up, but perhaps there was a little too much extra bulk around his middle. And while he was at it, his clothes were shabbier than they should have been. The hem of his jacket was starting to fray. Perhaps Piper would have some time to fix— No, Piper barely had time to put up her hair in the mornings, let alone mend his clothes on top of the kids'.

Athos shook his head. "I wish I had time to play baseball, but the train schedule is full and I only have so many hands and hours in the day. I can barely get home for supper every night as it is. I couldn't ask Piper to give up her few free hours just so I could play baseball now and then."

"Yes, but do you have *any* free hours?" Charlie asked, studying Athos and rubbing his chin.

Athos laughed. "No, no I haven't had free time for, oh, nearly ten years now. After the fourth was born, Natalie and I barely had time to say hello to each other, there was so much to do. And of course it's four times busier now. I don't know what I'd do if I didn't have Piper. The whole house would come crashing down."

As if on cue, there was a loud rip, then a crash, and a trio of female screams. The men jerked and twisted, looking for the cause of the disturbance.

Across the yard, one corner of the tent covering the tables of food had come down. Underneath it was a pile of silk and lace, petticoats and tablecloths. And more than a few splattered plates of buttered peas, cherry cordial, and apple pie. The screams had come from the four women who had been knocked over and splashed with bright red and greasy green. They struggled to get up, dresses ruined, gloves stained, and faces smeared with the spoiled part of the feast.

It would have been an alarming curiosity to Athos…if it wasn't Lael, Geneva, Millicent, and Thomas standing around the disaster with wide eyes and dirty hands.

"Oh, no." Athos winced and rushed toward the scene, along with the men he'd been talking to, most notably Rex Bonneville. It was his daughters who had ended up as the victims of the accident.

"Papa! Papa!" one, or maybe two of them, screamed. It was hard to tell which young ladies were talking underneath all the frills of skirts and underthings, tablecloths, and tent. "Help!"

Several men jumped forward to extract the Bonneville sisters from each other and from the remains of the table. Vivian Bonneville leapt into her father's arms as soon as she was free, squashing half an apple pie between them. Melinda and Bebe Bonneville were helped to their feet—both in tears—and immediately set about picking remnants of peas and pie crust off of what were undoubtedly expensive dresses. Solomon Templesmith reached down to help the last sister, Honoria, to stand. Honoria had been at the bottom of the pile, and although she'd escaped most of the food, she looked decidedly flattened and unwell, and broke into a coughing fit.

"Are you going to be all right, Miss Honoria?" Solomon asked, his arms still half around her to help with her balance.

Honoria coughed and pressed a hand to her pale face, then nodded.

"Get your hands off my daughter," Rex snapped.

"Rex," Bonnie tried to both scold and soothe him.

Rex ignored her, grabbing Honoria's arm and yanking her away. He caused her to lose her balance and almost stumble into the remaining mess on the grass. Rex didn't notice. He was too busy snapping at Solomon. "Who do you think you are? Money doesn't make you any less of a trained monkey."

Solomon straightened his tailored suit, fixed his dark eyes on Rex, and held himself with more dignity than Athos could ever have mustered. But as soon as he opened his mouth to protest, he was cut off.

"It was terrible, Papa," Vivian wailed. She shifted her stance to stand in such a way that the most people could hear her as she went on. "Those ragged little mongrels charged at us out of nowhere." She thrust out her arm and pointed dramatically at Lael, Geneva, Millicent, and Thomas.

Athos gathered his kids into a tight group around him, resting his hands on Neva and Millie's heads as if that could protect them. "I'm sure they didn't mean anything by it, did you?"

"No, Papa," they answered.

"We were being a train," Lael said.

"A runaway train," Geneva answered, eyes flashing with excitement. "The brave stationmaster was trying to save us by switching the tracks and preventing certain doom."

A grin tickled Athos's lips. Ever since they'd read the phrase 'certain doom' in a dime novel after supper the week before, Geneva had been using it in all of her games. "Is that so?"

"Yes, we—"

"Those children are a public menace," Melinda

yelped, cutting off Geneva's explanation. "They should be locked in the town jail."

"They should be hung, drawn, and quartered," Bebe added.

"They should be sent off to darkest Africa," Melinda went on.

"Yes, and fed nothing but gruel and roasted rats," Bebe finished.

If they had hoped to frighten the Strong children, they were sorely disappointed. From Lael down to Thomas, they all laughed.

"Roasted rats! Roasted rats!" Little Thomas shouted.

"What's going on here?" Piper came running to join the scene from the other side of the tent. She pulled up short when she saw the Bonneville sisters covered in food and stained with grass and cherry cordial. "Good heavens above." Before she could stop herself, she burst into laughter, then slapped a hand over her mouth.

"Vagrants, the lot of you!" Vivian shouted. "No good, pitiful, filthy vagrants."

"Now see here." Athos stepped forward, intending to defend his children to the death if he had to.

His attempt was cut short by a cracking boom and a high-pitched whiz several yards beyond the tent. Several ladies screamed. A half-second later, there was a sharp fizzle, then the opposite corner of the church tent caught fire. Another rash of screaming followed as women and children dashed out from under the tent and Dr. Dean Meyers and Aiden Murphy grabbed several glasses of lemonade to throw on the canvas. The fire went out quickly, which shifted everyone's focus to the cause of the sudden conflagration.

It wasn't difficult to find the culprits. Hubert stood with a box of matches in one hand and a burnt-out stub in the other. At his feet was a stick—the kind fireworks were attached to in order to assure a straight launch. Freddy and Noah stood several feet back. All three boys wore startled expressions on their pale faces.

"Vagrants!" Vivian called, even louder. "The younger ones tried to murder me and my sisters, and the oldest tried to burn down the—EEK!"

Her tirade came to an abrupt halt as Vernon rushed into the crowd to see what was going on, a grass snake in each hand. It was the Bonneville sisters' bad luck that he squeezed between Vivian and Melinda to get a good view of the fuss. Only, Vivian's shriek shocked him just enough for him to simultaneously jump and let go of the snakes. One fell on the ground and slithered under Bebe's skirts, but the other leapt right for Melinda's bosom. It just so happened that with her bodice sticky with apple pie, the snake stuck to her for the split-second it took for her to clap a hand to her chest in fright. The snake used that split-second to wriggle against her hand and up through the row of buttons on the front of the dress, disappearing under the fabric.

The shriek that erupted from Melinda was loud enough to wake the dead. "Get it off me, get it off me!" She bolted from the crumpled side of the tent in hysterics, ripping at her bodice.

Two of Bonneville's ranch hands chased after her and began helping relieve her of her bodice by tearing through it. It was only when the snake plopped to the ground and raced away that Melinda realized two rough men had divested her of part of her clothes. She let out an even more piercing scream and slapped the one closest to her with a resounding smack.

Bebe, meanwhile, had broken into a flat-out run, wailing in misery, "It's in my petticoats! Help! Help!" as she took herself as far as possible from the spot of grass her snake had landed in.

"This is an outrage," Rex Bonneville boomed. He advanced on Athos, fist raised.

Athos's first and only reaction was to throw both arms wide to shield his children. "It was an accident."

"Vivian is right," Bonneville went on. "Those children are conniving, evil-minded, wretches."

"They are not!"

"They're no better than beggars in the street, and you, sir, are unfit to be a father to them."

"Rex, calm down," Bonnie hissed from the side. She was ignored.

All of the grit and energy Athos had saved up to defend his children deflated under Bonneville's comment. As much as it hurt, the man might have had a point.

"My brother does the best he can," Piper stepped in to defend him. "He's a good father and a hard worker."

"Ha!" Bonneville barked.

His exclamation was underscored by Vivian's weeping and Melinda's and Bebe's continued shrieking as they fled the scene. Honoria—who had been standing by Solomon's side, watching the scene with wary eyes— hesitated, then rushed after them.

"You'll regret this," Vivian shouted, pointing a cherry cordial-stained finger at Athos. "The whole pathetic lot of you will regret this! Tell them, Papa." She didn't wait for her father to speak. She lifted her ruined skirts and fled after her sisters.

"You *will* regret this," Bonneville vowed in a far more menacing voice. He narrowed his eyes at Athos, taking one last threatening step toward him, then turned and stormed off, head held high.

"Sorry," Bonnie apologized on behalf of them all,

then picked up her skirts and chased after Bonneville with stooped shoulders.

A deep, awkward silence followed their departure. Athos's face pinched ruefully as he watched the man go. Rex Bonneville was a terrible man to make an enemy of. This was bad news all around. Incredibly bad news. He rubbed a hand over his face, then turned to face his four youngest.

"We're in trouble now," he told them as if he was one of them, another child waiting for the real adult to show up and scold them all. "Very bad trouble."

"We're sorry, Papa," Millie said, her eyes round and regretful. "We were just playing."

"We didn't even see misses Bonnevilles there," Geneva added.

Athos's heart broke at the sorrowful cast to their eyes. "No, sweethearts," he sighed. "You never do mean to get into trouble, do you?"

"No." The four young ones shook their head and looked down.

"Am I in trouble too, Papa?" Vernon asked, shuffling over to join his siblings. "They were only snakes, after all. Not even venomous ones."

Athos sighed and ruffled Vernon's hair. "I know." He looked up, searching outside of the ring of people who had gathered to watch with either sympathetic expressions or disapproving scowls. Many of them were helping right the table that had been upset, picking up the knocked-over tent pole, or assessing the firecracker's damage to the side of the tent canvas. Beyond that group, Hubert stood with his friends, being scolded roundly by Howard Haskell. Athos was glad he couldn't hear it. Then again, if he could, maybe he'd have half a clue what to say to his son. The only members of the family who had come out of the excitement unscathed were Ivy and Heather, but neither of them looked particularly eager to lay claim to the name Strong at the moment, as they hid their faces in their hands on the church stairs and were comforted by their friends.

"That's it!" The exasperated exclamation came from none other than Piper. She marched up to stand in front of Athos and the five children who hadn't escaped the disaster. "Athos, you're my brother and I love you, but you can't go on like this."

"Go on like what?" He could pretend innocence all he wanted, but Athos knew exactly where Piper's frustrated outburst was going.

"You're only one man," Piper went on. "And even though I'm your sister and would lay down my life for you, I need to have a life in order to lay it down in the first place."

"What are you talking about?" Athos reached out to grasp Millie's hand on one side and Neva's on the other. They squeezed his hands in return, apparently also realizing where this was going.

"How do you expect me to start a millinery business when I am forever minding my nieces and nephews? I love them, but I need a life too. And Mama keeps writing for me to come back home to Connecticut for a visit," Piper went on, losing some of her steam. "I haven't been home in three years, Athos. I have friends there, a life."

"I know that, Piper, and I've never forced you to stay with us or stopped you from visiting."

"I know." Piper pressed a hand to her temple. "But how was I supposed to leave you alone with all eight of them? I had hoped there would be some nice young woman in town, but…" She paused and sighed, shaking her head, then meeting Athos's eyes. "Natalie has been gone for four years, Athos. These children need a mother. A full-time mother who can devote her life to them. I love you all," she said to the children, "but I need a break. Athos, I'm putting my foot down. You need to remarry."

"I know, Piper, I know." Athos let his shoulders drop. Hadn't he been saying the same thing for the last several months? Everyone from Franklin Haskell to Travis Montrose seemed to be sending for a bride from Hurst Home. He had declared several times that he would do the same, but something had always come up. The station was always busy, his children always needed some sort of attention, and between those two things, there simply wasn't room for anything else.

"I think I see what's needed here," Charlie Garrett— who had stood close by watching the entire scene—spoke up. He gestured for Athos and Piper and the children to walk with him out of the way of the men and women who had swooped in to clean up the mess that had become of the tent. As soon as they were all a good ten yards out into the open yard beside the church, Charlie went on. "You need a bride from Hurst Home."

"Yes!" Athos let out the single word with so much weary emotion that it caused his throat to close up. A moment later, he shook himself. "I mean, I don't know. I...I wasn't a very good husband the first time. What reason do I have to believe that I'll be any good at it a second time?"

"No, Papa, no," Neva and Millie disagreed with him in unison.

"You're a great husband." Vernon too tried to bolster his spirits.

Athos laughed and ruffled Vernon's hair again. "And how would you know that?"

"Because you're the best Papa ever?" Lael replied.

Something not too unlike tears stung at Athos's eyes. He cleared his throat to fight the sensation. A good father—and a good husband—would be stronger than his emotions. He'd be organized and conscientious. He'd keep his children out of trouble and dress them, well, better than his poor things were dressed.

The oldest three children must have sensed something was in the air as Athos, Piper, and Charlie moved to the side. Hubert rushed to join the group, and even Ivy and Heather broke away from their friends long enough to gather with the rest of the family.

"What's going on?" Hubert asked.

"Papa is going to get a new bride," Vernon answered.

"Are you, Papa?" Heather asked.

"I...I..."

"He is," Charlie answered for him. "And your Aunt Piper is going to take a nice, restoring vacation back home in Connecticut."

"Yay!" Thomas exclaimed, although at four years old, Athos doubted he knew what he was cheering for.

"Mr. Garrett here is going to send for a bride for your father," Piper picked up the explanation. "I'm sure he knows exactly how it's done."

"Not only that," Charlie continued. He tilted his head to the side and tapped a finger to his chin. "I think I might know just the right woman for you."

"Really?" Athos blinked. The entire concept of the right woman for him was so foreign to his way of thinking that the idea that someone else would know of one mystified him.

"Yes." Charlie waved across the lawn to Virginia Piedmont and Josephine Evans.

The two of them stood somewhat aside from the

crews that were cleaning up the tent, as if sensing they would soon be needed elsewhere. At Charlie's signal, they made a bee-line across the lawn to join the ever-increasing group.

"Well, Charlie," Virginia started. "If you're the one waving at us and this lot are the ones you're talking to as you wave, I have one guess what this is all about."

"Especially after that display," Josephine agreed. She bent to pinch Thomas's chubby cheeks.

"You've finally decided to really, truly, and actually send for a wife, haven't you?" Virginia asked.

"Yes." Athos wished he didn't feel so defeated as he said it. This was a good thing for everyone, after all. He wasn't making the decision lightly, and judging by the smiles his friends and even his children wore, it was the right thing.

"I was thinking Elspeth Leonard," Charlie said.

"Who?" Athos turned to him.

"Yes," Josephine exclaimed, clapping her hands. "She *would* be perfect, wouldn't she?"

"Why, I can't think of a single other woman who would be more suited to the job of Mrs. Strong than Elspeth Leonard," Virginia agreed. "Good idea, Charlie."

"Who is Elspeth Leonard?" A tiny spark of hope had ignited in Athos's chest at the amount of enthusiasm his friends were showing.

"Elspeth Leonard is one of the women currently living at Hurst Home," Charlie explained. "She's been there for a little over a year. Mrs. Breashears has been giving me updates on the histories and talents of each of the women under her care so that we might assist her in placing them in Haskell."

"Elspeth is British," Virginia rushed on, evidently impatient with Charlie's storytelling pace. "British, though she's been in this country for the past seven years, working as a nanny and governess."

"Not only does Mrs. Breashears report she's quick and intelligent, she has experience caring for children," Josephine finished, eyes bright with excitement.

"She'd be our nanny?" Ivy asked, exchanging a confused look with her twin.

"No, she'd be your new mother, in a manner of speaking," Charlie went on. "She'd come out here to marry your father."

"But with the understanding that she is needed to care for the lot of you as well," Virginia finished.

A stunned silence followed. Athos turned to his children with a shrug. "Well, what do you think?"

"A new mama?" Millicent asked.

"Is she pretty?" Lael followed her question with one of his own.

"Is she nice?" Geneva asked her question as if she considered it to be most important.

"Yes, I should hope so, and of course," Charlie answered all three questions at once, then winked at the girls.

The girls giggled. The oldest three children turned to Athos, their expressions approving. Thomas swayed closer to his papa and took Athos's hand.

"What do you say, Athos?" Charlie asked. "I can telegraph Mrs. Breashears today, and if Miss Leonard is willing, she could be in Haskell as your bride by May first."

Athos studied his children, marked each one of their faces, looking for approval. He checked on Piper, who nodded in encouragement. Most of all, he searched his heart, wondering what Natalie would have said. She probably would have said that the children should have a mother…and he probably wouldn't have heard her as he rushed to get something else done or fix some other mistake.

Oh, Natalie. He sighed. The others would try to scold him and tell him he was wrong, but he really had been a terrible, absent-minded, inattentive husband. Miss Elspeth Leonard deserved better than his sorry bag of bones.

But he was desperate. In the end, only one thing mattered. His children needed a mother.

"All right." He gave up with a shrug. "Send the telegram. We'll do everything we can to get ready for Miss Elspeth Leonard."

Chapter Two

The train whistle squealed, jolting Elspeth out of her all-consuming thoughts. She hadn't felt the train slowing, so it came as something of a surprise to find the vast wilderness of Wyoming giving way to a growing town outside her window. Throughout the train car, people were standing to retrieve their bags and ready themselves to disembark.

"Haskell! Haskell, Wyoming!" The porter at the far end of the car called out.

Elspeth sucked in a breath, pressing a hand over her wriggling stomach. There was a family out there who needed her. Eight children was a lot, but she was up to the challenge. This was the right decision. This *had* to be the right decision. After more than half a decade of truly deplorable decisions, one of them had to be right.

She smoothed her gloved hands over her skirt and stood, scooting into the aisle so that she could retrieve her carpetbag from the rack above the seat. Her mother certainly wouldn't think risking everything to move out into the middle of the American frontier to marry a man sight unseen was a good decision. She would lecture Elspeth about how, as the daughter of a marquis, she was destined for much better things. Although Elspeth failed to see how being maneuvered into marrying some titled lord that she might have danced with once or twice in order to secure someone's line or fortune was any worse of a decision than becoming a mail-order bride. What her mother didn't know wouldn't hurt her…and seeing as Elspeth's entire family had completely severed ties with her five years ago, she never would know.

The train whistle shrieked a final time as the train jerked to a stop. The writhing in Elspeth's stomach grew. Thinking about the family that had disowned her wasn't going to help her face the family that waited for her in this remote, new town. The past was the past, and any sort of step she took to get away from it was a step in the right direction.

"Need help there, missy?" the porter asked as Elspeth adjusted the grip on her carpetbag.

"No, thank you, sir." She nodded, back straight, chin as high as she felt she deserved to lift it.

The porter's brow flew up. "Not from around these parts are you, ma'am?"

Undoubtedly, he was referring to what was left of her English accent, but she answered, "I am lately from Nashville, Tennessee."

The porter chuckled. "Well, you don't sound like any Tennessean I've ever heard." He stepped out of her way, extending an arm toward the front of the car as if inviting Elspeth on a stroll through Hyde Park. "Best of luck, ma'am."

"And you as well." She tried to smile as she nodded at the man. He continued to chuckle, probably at her manners this time. Some habits refused to leave a person, though. Her governess had taught her deportment when she was young, and for the past six years, she'd been attempting to teach it to the children she was hired to tutor.

Elspeth would have been much more confident in her abilities if any of those children had taken to her lessons. She squared her shoulders and marched toward the train car's door. Perhaps the Strong children would be well-mannered souls who would soak up the lessons of her childhood the way she and her siblings had instead of being grubby little rascals. It wasn't that she disliked her previous charges, but with no references, a dubious history, and nothing to distinguish her aside from an accent that Americans considered distinguished, the only families she'd found work with were social-climbing new money with one foot still in the gutter or the back alley.

The Strong family would be different. Mrs. Breashears had assured her of it. Elspeth turned to step down from the train car and onto the platform with hope in her heart. This time, she really would make a go of things, really would start over. Mr. Athos Strong came highly recommended after all, and she was marrying him, not entering his employment. This time, things would—

"That's her! I know that's her," a child shouted.

"She looks just like Mrs. Breashears said she would," a second, older child added.

"Hurray! Hurray for our new mother!" a third whooped.

More young shouts followed, and before Elspeth could get her bearings and assess the situation, a mob of eight children rushed her. Four or five of the youngest of the bunch slammed into her, nearly knocking her off her feet as they hugged, grabbed, and clutched her.

Elspeth yelped before she could stop herself. She

dropped her bag and was bowled back several feet by the clinging crowd of happy youngsters.

"Your dress is so soft!"

"You're just as pretty as I knew you'd be."

"I'm going to be your favorite, I just know it."

"Papa, Papa! Come and look!"

A chorus of voices and motion buzzed around her as Elspeth panted to catch her breath.

"You *vagrants* step back and leave her alone," a slightly older girl scolded the younger ones.

"Papa, they're going to smother her," a second girl, who looked to be the first one's twin, added.

Elspeth scrambled to remember the list of names Mrs. Breashears had given her. The twins must be Ivy and Heather. The littlest one—presently clinging to her skirt—was Thomas. The second set of twin girls were Geneva and Millicent. That meant the two boys who had hugged her and backed off must be Lael and Vernon, and the young man who stood on the fringes of the group wearing a grin on his pimply face must be Hubert. Good gracious! A paper list of names was one thing. A crush of children was another.

"Sorry, sorry, sorry." An older woman in a moss-green riding dress with a fetching hat perched on her silver hair stepped forward, wedging her way between the children. "This lot always has been...exuberant. I'm Virginia Piedmont."

Virginia thrust out her hand with as much exuberance as any of the children.

"Isn't she pretty, Mrs. Piedmont?" one of the younger twin girls asked.

"Did somebody pick up her bag?" the boy who must have been Vernon shouted.

"Will you read me a story?" Thomas asked, eyes as big as moons.

"I...I..."

"Children, step back. Give Miss Leonard some air."

The final command was given by a man who stood on the edges of the scene wearing a stationmaster's uniform. He crushed a round, black hat in his hands and shifted his weight from foot to foot as he looked on. His sandy-blond hair framed a round face with soft, hazel eyes. Elspeth had hardly noticed him, but she knew in an instant that he must be Athos Strong. Her husband-to-be.

"Do as your papa says and give Miss Leonard some space," Virginia declared. She shooed the kids as if they were cattle, with a bright smile and a teasing wink. As soon as they'd all backed up by several feet—Thomas only stepping away unwillingly from where he had grabbed onto Elspeth's skirt—Virginia let out a happy breath. "Welcome to Haskell."

At last, an interaction that had some sort of context in Elspeth's experience. She belatedly took Virginia's hand. "Thank you. I am most pleased to be here."

"Ooh, did you hear the way she talks, Papa?" the other of the younger twin girls asked, turning to her father.

"Yes, I did, sweetness." Athos smiled and rested a hand on his daughter's head.

A small portion of the tension that had been growing in Elspeth's whole body released. Athos smiled at his daughter, at all of his children, with such kindness and affection that emotion squeezed her throat. Her own parents would never have dared show such attention in public. Anyone who showed that much consideration for children must be a gentleman, and she was not afraid to marry a gentleman. Not after being buffeted about by so many un-gentlemanly men.

"Well then," Virginia went on, throwing up her hands. "The timing of this whole introduction has been blown to smithereens, so there's no point in beating around the bush. Elspeth Leonard, I'd like you to meet Athos Strong. Athos, here's Elspeth, your bride."

Virginia stepped out of the way, clearing the space between Elspeth and Athos. Elspeth stiffened her spine and called on all of her courage to face the man she'd pledged to marry. Only instead of marching up to her and laying claim on her in any way, Athos Strong stood where he was, a bashful flush coming to his cheeks and a warm smile lighting his face. Another measure of the anxiety that the entire journey had built up in Elspeth melted away. The man was shy.

"Go on, Papa," one of the older twins whispered.

"She's waiting," the second twin added.

Together, the two of them pushed against his back, causing Athos to take a faltering step forward. The other children giggled.

That simple action seemed to break the spell. Athos cleared his throat and shook himself, then walked amiably forward, extending his hand. "I'm very pleased to meet you, Miss Leonard."

Once again, Elspeth found herself on familiar footing. She could do this. She'd met new men in ballrooms and drawing rooms across London all the time. She could greet a widowed father on a train platform on the frontier.

"Call me Elspeth, please." She took his hand with her gloved one and began to execute a perfect curtsy before grasping how inappropriate that was. "We are to be married, after all."

"Yes." Athos's expression lit even more. He tightened

his hand around hers in a handshake that showed his strength and his tenderness. After he let go of her hand, he continued to smile at her without moving.

"I think Papa likes her," the younger of the two middle boys, Lael, whispered.

"I like her," Thomas said in full voice.

Athos laughed and backed up, shaking himself out of whatever thoughts he'd had. "Miss—Elspeth, I'd like you to meet my pride and joy, my brood of scamps and ruffians."

"Papa!"

"We are not!"

"No fair!" The children protested, laughing.

"This is my eldest, Hubert." Athos crossed to the other side of the cluster of children to the young man with pimples. He then turned to the older set of twins. "And these are my little ladies, Ivy and Heather. This one over here is Vernon." He moved on to ruffle the next boy's hair. "And this is Lael. These two misses are Geneva and Millicent." He squeezed each of their shoulders as he named them. "And this little ragamuffin is Thomas."

"I'm the youngest," Thomas announced, then shot on into, "My mama died when I was born."

Tension seized the entire group. It gradually dissolved as Athos laughed nervously. "I'm sure there will be plenty of time to talk about that later. But right now, I believe Rev. Pickering is expecting us over at the church. Are you ready?"

"Yes!"

"We are!"

"Let's go!" The children rang out in chorus.

"He was asking Miss Leonard," Hubert informed the others.

Another chorus of, "Ohh," followed.

In spite of the shock of the situation, Elspeth laughed. They truly were a sweet bunch of children, even if they did come at her like a hurricane.

"You may call me Elspeth as well," she told them, clasping her hands in front of her as she did when she was teaching.

"Not Mama?" Millicent asked.

Elspeth blinked, startled. "Well…I…I suppose…" She glanced to Athos for help.

"Let's head over to the church first and we'll figure out the rest of it later," he said. "Elspeth?" He offered his arm as if he wasn't used to escorting women and wasn't sure that was still the way things were done. He didn't seem to know what to say to her either.

The children rushed ahead of them and lingered behind, chattering to each other, chasing after a dog that they were apparently friends with who had trotted by the platform to see what was going on, and ran this way and that. There was so much motion and commotion that Elspeth's head spun. She supposed she should ask about her luggage, whether it would be removed from the train, or whether Athos had stationmaster duties he should attend to since the train was there, but a pair of non-uniformed men seemed to be taking care of things. Virginia walked with them, but her attention was taken up as Ivy and Heather asked her about horses.

They had traveled half the distance to the whitewashed church set back from the tracks and surrounded by a well-maintained yard, and Elspeth still couldn't think of a thing to say.

"Afternoon, Athos," a handsome man in a buckskin vest with a sly look called out as they passed. He stood talking to a handsomely-dressed but sad-looking woman.

"Morning, Sam, Bonnie," Athos replied with a wave.

The sad woman, Bonnie, smiled, the smile not quite reaching her eyes. "Is this your mail-order bride, arrived at last?"

Athos paused long enough to say, "Yes it is. This is Miss Elspeth Leonard. Elspeth, this is Miss Bonnie Horner, who owns the, uh, um, an establishment in town."

"How do you do?" Elspeth greeted the woman, ignoring her confusion at the way Athos had introduced her. Going by his words alone, Bonnie should be someone disreputable, but she was dressed as conservatively as a preacher's wife and no one seemed to bat an eye at her.

"I do just fine, Miss Leonard," Bonnie answered.

"And this is Sam Standish," Athos went on. "He owns the town's saloon."

"Ma'am." Sam touched the brim of his hat.

"Mr. Standish." Elspeth inclined her head to him.

"Did that train bring my shipment of whiskey?" Sam asked.

"Uh." Athos twisted to look over his shoulder. "You'll have to ask Travis and Freddy. They're unloading it for me. I've got a…well—" He glanced at Elspeth and grinned. "We're due at the church," Athos said, then continued down the street. The children and Virginia had slipped ahead of them, and Athos hurried as if he should keep up.

"I hope it doesn't bother you that I'm friends with people like Bonnie and Sam," he continued as they walked.

"Bother me? Why should it?" Elspeth blinked.

"Well, most respectable woman—like Mrs. Kline at the mercantile or the Plovers or the Bonneville sisters— don't think it's right to associate with a saloon owner or a whoremonger." He missed a step, his face going red.

"Sorry. I shouldn't be using language like that around you."

Elspeth nodded slowly. So that's what Bonnie's profession was. A flush of her own splashed Elspeth's cheeks. Her mother would have insisted she shun that sort of woman, but when it came down to it, Elspeth didn't have a moral leg to stand on there. At least Haskell was accepting of people of all sorts.

"I don't mind." She summarized her complex thoughts in one simple sentence.

Athos's shoulders relaxed. "I'm glad. We're all good people here in Haskell, make no mistake. Howard Haskell founded the town about ten years ago, and it's developed into an interesting place."

"Interesting?" Elspeth peeked around, but the buildings and streets, the passersby and the wagons, didn't seem any different from any other town she'd tried to make a new start in.

"Howard insists that economic prosperity comes from embracing *everyone's* talents, no matter where they come from or what sort of life they lived before. The only things he disapproves of are idleness, pettiness, and stinginess. Everything else…" He finished his statement with a shrug.

"I should like to meet Howard Haskell," Elspeth said.

"I'm sure you will before too long," Athos continued. "And half the rest of the town. Everyone has been eager to see me married off again. I mean—" He rushed to qualify his statement before he'd even taken a breath. "Folks around here know how difficult it's been to manage eight children and hold down a job running Haskell's train station."

"I can imagine."

"The job has grown with the town, and I haven't had

the time to sit down and figure out ways to make it easier on myself. Not that I'm complaining, mind you. I believe in doing the job you've been given to the best of your ability without complaint. So I do. Trains come through nearly every day loaded with supplies, passengers, you name it. Someone's got to organize it all."

"But what about your family? Who organizes them?"

"My sister, Piper, has been helping out, but she headed back home to Connecticut for a visit just the day before yesterday. Don't worry, she's coming back to Haskell, but probably not until August."

The most polite thing to say to that was, "I'm sure you look forward to her return."

"Of course." Athos grinned. "But I have you now." He blinked, and his grin dropped. "I mean...that's not to say...I don't think of you as a sister. Or...or as hired help. Even though it will be helpful to have you around."

"I understand, Mr. Strong." Elspeth sent him a reassuring smile, patting his arm.

"Athos. Please," he corrected her, color splashing his cheeks.

"I understand, Athos, that you didn't simply send for me as a caretaker for the children." As soon as the words were out, a horrible thought struck her and she nearly missed a step. "You didn't, did you?"

A look of horror came into his eyes. "Oh, dear me, no!" He laughed. "I'm sorry if you got that impression."

"I...I don't know what impression to have."

"It's not just a worker that I, that we all were hoping for. It's someone to lean on. To befriend. Raising children is more than just cooking meals and scrubbing faces. It's being there to give hugs, listening to problems, and sharing a few words of advice and support when needed."

Prickles broke out on Elspeth's skin at his description. Instinct told her that while he may have needed those things for his children, he also needed them for himself. She took a closer look at him as they walked on. His expression was kind and eager to please, and he waved and nodded when they crossed paths with neighbors. Did he know that he needed the kind of emotional support he apparently wanted for his children? Mrs. Breashears said he was a special man in need of a special wife. Perhaps she wasn't just being glib after all.

They reached the churchyard as he finished only to be greeted by a round of shrieks of excitement and cries of "Papa! Yay! Yay for Elspeth!" The dog that some of the children had chased from the platform was barking and frolicking as Vernon, Lael, and Thomas chased it. At some point between the station and the church Thomas must have tripped, because his clothes were covered with grass stains and dirt.

"How on earth…" Athos began, but let the question drop as Geneva and Millicent dashed around the corner of the church.

"Papa! Papa! Look, we've picked flowers for you and for Elspeth!"

The girls skidded to a stop at the bottom of the stairs, practically tossing a bouquet of wildflowers at Elspeth. She caught it with fumbling hands, then did what any polite lady would do and lifted it to her face to sniff.

Immediately, a bee took off from its perch on one of the flowers. Elspeth yelped and threw the bouquet away on instinct, then felt terrible as the flowers scattered to the ground.

"I'm sorry. I'm so sorry," she apologized to the girls.

"Don't worry," Millicent smiled.

"We'll pick you another one," Geneva added. She

grabbed her sister's hand and the two of them tore off around the corner of the church.

"We'd better go inside." Athos took Elspeth's hand and started up the stairs with her.

"Me too, me too!" Thomas called, lifting his arms as if he wanted to be picked up. He settled for Athos grabbing one of his hands and helping him up the stairs.

The inside of the church took Elspeth's breath away. Stained glass windows ran up and down the sides, and with the afternoon light streaming through them, the interior of the church was awash with color. It was light and airy, and the pulpit and chancel at the front were clean and tidy. The high ceiling also served to amplify sound, particularly the high-pitched squeals and shouts of Vernon and Lael as they ran inside the church. With the dog.

"Boys! Get Mr. Tremaine's dog back outside," Athos called out. He let go of Elspeth's hand and joined his sons in trying to catch and subdue the dog.

"Papa! Keep him away from here," Heather shouted from the front of the church. She and Ivy were busy arranging flowers near the front pews.

The dog darted between two of the pews, Vernon and Lael followed, laughing loud. There was a thump as a pile of hymnals in the row was knocked over, then another crash as Vernon leapt over the back of the pew and landed half on the dog, half on a second pile of hymnals.

"What on earth is going on back there?" Virginia glanced up from where she had been talking to a man in a plain suit on the chancel. Elspeth imagined he must be Rev. Pickering.

"No, no, no! Boys, what are you doing?" The reverend broke away from Virginia and rushed down the aisle.

"We're chasing Bo," Lael informed him with a shout, skittering into the aisle.

Bo the dog evidently knew the game was up if Rev. Pickering was involved. Tongue lolling out the side of his mouth, he bounded toward the back of the church, scrambling out through the open church door. Vernon and Lael attempted to follow him, but they reached the door just as Geneva and Millicent were coming in. Lael slammed into Millicent, knocking her flat on her back in the doorway.

"Oh dear," Athos sighed as Millicent burst into tears. He rushed to her, scooping her into his arms and simultaneously comforting her and looking for injuries.

"He broke my flowers," Millicent wailed.

"It's okay, I picked them up," Geneva tried to console her. "We have enough."

"Sorry, Millie," Lael apologized as his sister was talking.

"There, Lael said he was sorry, and we didn't even have to remind him." Athos set Millicent on her feet, but kept his arms around her as she continued to weep. "You're all right. Just a little startled."

"My flowers!"

"I've got some right here."

"We've got more at the front," Ivy called from the chancel.

Elspeth could only stand where she was, utterly stunned. Within the course of three minutes she'd witnessed at least five disasters. Half of the kids continued to chatter away, reassuring Millicent that everything would be all right or asking Rev. Pickering questions.

"Can I give away the bride?"

"Is a wedding magic?"

"Will Papa really be married to Elspeth just by saying 'I do?'"

Elspeth's head spun with the whirlwind around her. She wasn't entirely sure how Athos managed to herd his entire brood up to the front of the church and her along with them, but she still hadn't completely gotten her bearings when Athos took her arm again and led her to stand in front of Rev. Pickering.

"We'll do the ceremony first, and then you can sign the certificate and go off to begin your life together." The reverend spoke with the tone of someone saying they'd finish up as fast as possible so that the kids could leave.

"Don't you need two witnesses to have a wedding?" Hubert asked, moving to stand by his father's side. He stood taller, grinning with expectation.

"I'm afraid you're too young to act as witness," Rev. Pickering informed him.

"I'll get you a witness, Papa." Ivy didn't wait for an answer, she tore off down the church aisle and outside.

Of course, half of her siblings needed to run with her, while the other half decided now was the time to clean up from the mess that the dog had left. In three seconds, the whirlwind had started up again.

"You'll get used to it," Athos told Elspeth, as good-naturedly as possible. "By eight, nine o'clock at night, they've simmered down."

"What time do they get up in the morning?" Elspeth asked.

"Oh, around six? Sometimes five."

"Oh dear."

Ivy rushed back into the church five minutes later, dragging a middle-aged lady who was introduced to Elspeth as Mrs. Olivia Garrett. Mrs. Garrett was not only the wife of Charlie Garrett—who Elspeth had heard all about at Hurst Home—she taught some of the children. She had a sense of humor about the whole affair, and once more, everyone took their places at the front of the church.

"Dearly beloved, we are gathered here today in the sight of God and these, our friends—"

"And me," Thomas added, raising his hand.

Rev. Pickering smiled. "And Thomas, to join this man and this woman in holy matrimony."

The service zipped by ten times faster than the journey to the church or the preparation for the wedding had. Halfway through, Geneva noticed she was still holding the bouquet of wildflowers intended for Elspeth, so proceedings were momentarily halted for the time it took to sort flowers out. Half of the children had to have a say in which flowers should be included in the bouquet and whether all of the girls should have flowers, but the actual recital of the vows and the 'I dos' were over in a blink.

"I now pronounce you man and wife," Rev. Pickering said. "You may kiss the bride."

"Papa, are you going to kiss her?" Lael asked, screwing up his face in disgust, before any action could be taken.

Athos laughed. "I suppose I am. If you don't mind."

Elspeth had always dreamed of kissing her husband as the minister pronounced them man and wife. A quick thrill of excitement swirled up in her, but it was blown off course by Geneva and Millicent hopping up and down and insisting, "Kiss Papa! Kiss Papa!"

"All right." She did her best to smile at the girls— they really were darling the way they cared for their father—and turned to face Athos.

A strange, far-away look came into Athos's eyes for a moment, almost like worry. Then he took a breath, rested a hand on Elspeth's arm, and leaned in for a kiss. Elspeth closed her eyes, letting his lips touch hers. A surprise rush of delight filled her as warmth and pressure, promise and hope filled her. It was more than just a quick peck, and something in the simple gesture pulled at her heart, leaving her wondering what it would be like to kiss Athos if they weren't surrounded by a mob.

"Huzzah!" the children shouted.

Athos pulled back, his expression startled. His gaze remained locked with Elspeth's for longer than she would have thought, and he smiled. That smile seeped right into her, once again filling her with the confidence that Athos Strong was a good man.

"If you'll just step this way, you can sign the certificate," Rev. Pickering interrupted.

"I want to sign a certificate too," Thomas piped up.

"You can't even write your name yet," Vernon teased him.

"I can too!"

"We have been practicing," Ivy informed Vernon, her nose in the air as if he was just another stupid boy.

"You have snot in your nose," Vernon said.

"I do not! Papa!"

"Settle down, kids, settle down," Athos laughed, herding the lot of them over to the table on the side where Rev. Pickering was waiting with a pen and a certificate. "Let's do this one last thing, then you can take Miss—I mean, Mrs. Elspeth Strong home and show her the house."

"*We* can take her?" Heather balked. Her surprise reflected Elspeth's own reaction.

Athos took the pen from Rev. Pickering, signed the certificate, then handed the pen to Elspeth. As she signed, he said, "I'm afraid I have to get back to work."

The children all moaned in protest. Elspeth finished

signing, then handed the pen to Olivia and looked to Athos for an explanation.

Athos shrugged. "The train just came in. Travis and Freddy can unload the cargo and baggage for me, but I'm the only one who can make sure the shipments are logged and inventoried and everything gets where it needs to be."

"Papa, you're always working," Millicent huffed, crossing her arms.

Elspeth was inclined to agree with the girl, and she'd only really known the man an hour or less. "Do you have some sort of assistant who can help you?"

"Me," Hubert spoke up. "I help after school."

Elspeth smiled at the young man, but she wasn't as reassured as she wanted to be.

"I keep telling you to ask Howard about hiring an assistant stationmaster," Virginia said as she passed them on her way to the door.

"I don't want anyone to have to go through any extra trouble on my account," Athos answered.

Elspeth wondered just how much trouble it could be to save yourself an even bigger amount of trouble.

"Maybe I'll talk to Howard," Athos said, gesturing for them all to head on out of the church. "In the meantime, I want you all to be perfect angels for Elspeth."

"Yes, Papa," the children answered.

"Show her where everything is kept and where all of your rooms are. We want to welcome her to her new home with open arms."

"Yes, Papa."

"We're all going to be one big, happy family, aren't we?"

Ivy and Heather answered, "Yes, Papa," but the rest of the children had torn out the back door and scattered across the churchyard.

Chapter Three

Three hours, two scraped knees, one screaming match between Geneva and Millicent and Lael and Vernon, a minor fire in the kitchen during supper preparation, and Elspeth was exhausted.

"Where is the milk pitcher?" Heather hollered from the dining room into the kitchen as she and Ivy set the table for supper.

"Um…" Elspeth twisted this way and that, searching the messy countertops. She hadn't had time to wash the mixing bowls or put away the flour and eggs and herbs that had been taken out to prepare enough chicken and biscuits to feed the hoard. The milking pail that Hubert had brought up from the root cellar earlier was still on the kitchen table, but it was empty. Elspeth crossed to the cupboard, opening one door after another to see if the pitcher was there. Cups and plates, platters and mugs were thrown into the cupboards willy-nilly, adding to the feeling of chaos.

Elspeth's heart raced as if she had hiked a mountain.

She turned to rest against the cupboard, fighting down the panic that so much disorder caused.

"I found it!" Ivy called out, coming into the kitchen from the hallway with the milk pitcher in her hands. "Somebody put it in the front parlor."

"Oh!" Lael glanced up from where he was cutting up carrots. "I put it there."

"Lael!" Ivy huffed, walking on to take the pitcher to the dining room.

"What?" Lael threw out his hands. "There was no place to put it in here."

Before Elspeth could say anything about that, the kitchen door smacked open and Geneva, Millicent, and Thomas rushed inside.

"Flowers! Flowers!" the girls shouted in unison. "We picked flowers for the table."

Joy and terror mingled in Elspeth's heart. Her head had been spinning since the moment she stepped off the train, but it wasn't truly the children's fault. They were helpful and lively. She'd experienced a moment of panic when she remembered her carpetbag but couldn't find it, only to have Hubert say he'd already taken it up to her room. Ivy and Heather had taken her on a tour of the house, then set to work helping her prepare for supper. Vernon and Lael had done their chores—sweeping the front porch, collecting eggs from the chickens in the coop out back, and helping gather laundry from each bedroom and taking it to the room at the back of the house which was designated for washing up of all kinds—and the youngest children had zipped about, trying to help their older siblings. But the very fact that the house had an entire room just for washing filled Elspeth with dread. Laundry days must be an event in the Strong house.

"Neva, Millie, are those flowers from Mrs. Evans's

garden?" Hubert asked, strolling into the kitchen through the back door.

Athos was right behind him, looking tired but smiling. His stationmaster uniform was rumpled, and he'd somehow acquired a stain on his sleeve. Elspeth straightened and sent a panicked look around the kitchen. He would probably think she was severely incompetent to have the place looking such a mess when he returned from work. But no, he didn't even blink at it.

"Mrs. Evans said we could pick them," Geneva rushed to defend herself.

"Did she say that *today*?" Hubert asked.

The girlish guilt in the twins' expressions was answer enough.

"Papa!" Thomas rescued his sisters by throwing out his arms and running at Athos.

"Thomas!" Athos replied in the same excited tone. He caught Thomas as he slammed into him, lifting the boy and hugging him. "Have you been good for Elspeth?"

"Yes." Thomas nodded.

"Papa, you're home!" Ivy and Heather ran into the kitchen from the dining room, rushing to hug their father and bring him further into the room.

"You're almost never home before we start supper," Lael observed. He gave his vegetables a few more chops, then went to give his father a hug too.

Elspeth's brow inched up. Her heart warmed to see the children greet their father with such affection, but at the same time, she felt like an outsider intruding on a family scene.

"I rushed to get everything taken care of with this afternoon's arrival," Athos explained, putting Thomas down and hugging each of his children in turn.

"And I helped," Hubert added, standing taller.

"So I'll be able to lead grace at supper tonight. Imagine that," Athos laughed.

He finished hugging his kids, then turned to Elspeth. All of his easy affection clammed up. A hint of color came to his face as he stood where he was, smiling uncertainly at Elspeth. His arms twitched as though he would reach out to hug her, but he held back. There was a sparkle of fondness in his eyes as he looked at her, but in the end, all he did was clear his throat.

"Have you had a pleasant afternoon?" he asked.

Elspeth indulged in her observations of him for a few seconds more. She couldn't decide if he was handsome or if the positive feelings she felt when she was around him came from his clear affection for his children. It was obvious that the children were everything to him.

"It was a busy afternoon," she answered at last. "But the children were helpful."

"I'm glad to hear it." He stayed where he was, his smile as fond and uncertain as ever. "Do you need any more help getting supper on the table?"

"I can carry plates," Vernon offered.

"I'll get the chicken," Ivy added.

"And I'll get the vegetables," Heather followed.

"The vegetables aren't finished yet." Lael stopped her from whisking his work away.

The moment of relative calm passed and the flurry of activity resumed. This time, all ten people were involved in setting the table, pouring glasses of milk, water, or in Athos's case, weak beer, getting the vegetables into the pot, taking potatoes out of the pot, baking another tray of biscuits, and basting the chicken several times before taking it out of the oven. Elspeth was grateful for the help, but the sheer volume of movement and noise as people chatted and shouted instructions to each other left her bewildered by the time they all moved to the dining room to sit down.

"You sit at the foot of the table," Millicent instructed her as the children all scrambled to take their places. "Papa sits at the head."

"If that's where you want to sit," Athos added as he sat at the head, Hubert on one side, Ivy and Heather on the other. The children arranged themselves from there in order from oldest to youngest. That left Elspeth sitting with Thomas on one side and Millicent on the other.

"This is perfect." Elspeth smiled as she sat.

No sooner had she tucked in her chair than the children and Athos all joined hands. Surprised, Elspeth reached tentatively for Thomas's and Millicent's hands. Everyone bowed their heads.

"Lord, for the food and good fortune you have given us, let us be truly thankful," Athos said.

The children began to chorus, "Ame—"

"Ah!" Athos stopped them. A rush of giggles followed, then Athos went on with, "And let us be thankful for Elspeth as well. We will love her and cherish her as one of our own."

Tears stung at Elspeth's eyes before the children could say a second, "Ame—"

"Ah!" Athos stopped them once again. More giggles sprang up, louder this time. "And let us remember to be good and obey what Elspeth says, and to pick up our dirty clothes and to put our toys away and brush our teeth before going to bed."

He paused. The children began a hesitant "A—" An expectant hush fell over the table. Elspeth opened one eye. Athos's eyes were still closed, but all around the table, the children were peeking at him and each other, and at her. A grin formed on Elspeth's lips, and a giggle caught in her throat. The tension that hung over the table with all the pent-up laughter was palpable.

"—men!" Athos shouted at last.

"Amen!" the children all cried out, then burst into laughter and dug into their supper.

Elspeth couldn't shake her smile as she carved her chicken—and cut up Thomas's as well. Family dinners of her childhood had consisted of her and her siblings eating in silence with their nanny in the nursery. On the few occasions she had dined with her parents, she'd been expected to sit still, to eat daintily, and to keep her mouth shut. The Strong's table was a sea of noise and confusion, and more than a few spills, but in one minute, with one blessing, Athos had made her feel more welcome and more…loved than her family ever had. It was beautiful, and it was overwhelming.

With a little encouragement from Athos, the children all helped clean up from supper once everyone had had their fill. The older girls helped Elspeth store the leftover food while the older boys helped the younger ones first with their homework and then washing up and changing for bed. As much as Elspeth wanted to tidy the kitchen and the dining room from top to bottom, there was only so much she could do before it was dark and all of the children needed to be readied for bed.

The kids had one major incentive to put on their nightclothes and wash their faces and brush their teeth. As Athos explained while the mad rush to use the washroom downstairs and one designated room upstairs was in full swing, the house rule was that if everyone was ready before the clock on the mantle downstairs struck nine, Athos would read to them. Elspeth was astounded by how vigilant the children were in getting ready for their treat. She was equally astounded by Athos's choice of reading material once they were all gathered in one of the bedrooms.

"Black Bart reached for the revolver in the holster at his hip," Athos read the lurid dime novel in a voice that left his children gasping in excitement. "'I reckon you better git,' Bart growled, stroking the handle of his revolver. Dirk Manley wasn't intimidated. He widened his stance, puffing out his chest to show his sheriff's star. 'This town won't be cowed by the likes of you anymore.'"

"Papa, what does 'cowed' mean?" Geneva asked.

"Did he turn him into a cow?" Lael attempted to supply an answer.

"No." Athos laughed. "It means intimidated or beaten down."

"So Dirk Manley won't let Black Bart push him around." Vernon nodded.

"Right." Athos reached over to ruffle his hair, then went on. "'We've got good on our side,' Dirk said. 'Evil never prospers.'"

Elspeth covered her mouth with one hand, half to hide her smile at the sweetness of the scene in front of her and half to stifle a yawn. It seemed like she'd arrived days ago instead of hours. The dime novel was thrilling, and the children gasped with each new twist that Athos read, but Elspeth could barely keep her eyes open.

When Athos finally ended the chapter on a cliff-hanger—causing the children to whine in protest and to beg for one more chapter, but to no avail—eight tired little bodies finally dragged themselves off to their own rooms. Ivy and Heather shared a room and hinted to Elspeth that they would stay up reading their own books for a little while longer. Hubert, surprisingly, shared a room with little Thomas and carried him off, already half asleep. The younger twins shared a room and Lael and Vernon shared the room which doubled as the upstairs wash room.

"I don't know how you managed to find places for them all," Elspeth commented through a yawn as she retired to her own room.

"It is tight," Athos agreed, following her. "But we've managed to make it work. There's a bit more room in the attic, but Piper has claimed that entire floor as her domain."

"Your sister lives in the attic?" Elspeth asked, lips twitching as she tried to decide if that was practical or mad-capped.

"She does," Athos chuckled. "She's made things much nicer up there than you would expect." He closed the door behind them, then shrugged out of his suspenders.

Shock coursed through Elspeth as he undressed. A second later she shook her head at her ridiculous reaction. Somewhere in the confusion of the day she'd forgotten that she and Athos were married. Of course they would share a room. She peeked at the bed out of the corner of her eye. Of course they would share a *bed*.

Heat flooded her face. She tried to shake that off as well. It wasn't as if she was some blushing virgin who had never known a man's touch. No, a man's touch was what had gotten her into this life in the first place. And even though Craig Valko had broken her heart and left her destitute in a foreign country, she was forced to admit she'd enjoyed her scandalous nights with him. At least at first. She reached for the buttons of her blouse, rolling her eyes at herself for her shaking hands. Athos was a good, kind man, as far from the man Craig turned out to be as possible. Pleasing him in bed was the least she could do for him.

Across the room, Athos stopped halfway through taking off his shirt. His eyebrows tipped up as he studied her, then he burst into chuckles as if he'd grasped the punchline to a joke. "No, no, no, don't worry about any of *that.*" He resumed undressing.

"A-any of what?" Elspeth winced at the tremor in her voice, but forced herself to continue removing her clothes.

"*That.*" Athos shook his head and unfastened his trousers. "I don't expect anything resembling..." He cleared his throat, a flush coming to his cheeks. "Anything like a wedding night, now or...or ever, if that's what you want."

"Oh?" Elspeth let her hands drop to her side.

"No." He stepped out of his trousers, folded them, and lay them across a chair on the other side of the room. Then he crossed back to the bed and pulled back the covers. "I'm exhausted after today, and I can only imagine how tired you are. I saw you yawning while I read *The Outlaw's Last Stand.*"

"I didn't mean to be rude." She shrugged out of her blouse, turning toward her trunk, which Hubert had set against the wall earlier. At some point, she would have to make time—and space—to put away her things.

"You weren't rude at all." Athos laughed as he settled on his back in the bed. "Eight children is entirely overwhelming. Piper usually goes up to her room to work on hats after supper. She has plans to start a millinery business, you know, and that's the only time she has to be alone. You're a good sport for staying up with us."

"It was my pleasure."

It felt a little odd to change into her nightgown with a man in a bed potentially watching her just a few feet away. When Elspeth turned to the bed, though, Athos was carefully looking away. Like a gentleman. As soon as she slid in beside him and pulled the covers up to her chin, he turned back to smile at her.

"Honestly, as wonderful as being married and sharing a bed as a married couple is, and as much as I enjoy sexual relations—" He paused, flushing. "That was probably more than you need to know."

"It's all right," Elspeth said, feeling herself flush. "I-I'm not a virgin."

He glanced up at her. He didn't look surprised. "As nice as all that is," he went on, "to tell you the truth, I haven't had two spare seconds to think about anything like that in ages. There's too much work, too many children to see to, too many trains. I didn't send for you only because I wanted someone to warm my bed."

"You sent because you needed someone to share your load." She realized the truth of it as she spoke.

Athos laughed and settled on his back. With a sleepy sigh he said, "These days I'm more of an automaton, put in motion to make sure everyone else is taken care of."

If there was more to his thought, he didn't speak it aloud, even though Elspeth waited. She didn't have to wait long before Athos's breathing turned steady and deep with sleep.

A strange sort of sadness filled her heart as she adjusted her position and stared up at the ceiling. An automaton was nothing more than a machine. There was something tragic about hearing the same man who had just spent a lovely evening with his children referring to himself as a machine. And yet, what could she do about it?

Athos slept like a rock and woke with a deep-seated confidence that everything would be all right from now on, that his children would be safe and healthy with Elspeth helping raise them, and that he might just be able to make a good friend of his new wife. It wasn't until he was out of bed, undressed, scrubbing himself down for the day with a sponge and the bowl of water on the table in the corner of his room that it dawned on him his new wife might have different standards of modesty than he did. With a wince, he glanced over his shoulder to see if she was still asleep.

"Sorry," he whispered when he found her staring fixedly at the wall, fully awake. He reached for the towel he kept draped over the chair beside the wash table, drying off then wrapping it around his waist. "You get used to seeing all sorts of things when you share a house with so many people," he chuckled.

"Oh? Oh, it's not that." Elspeth's cheeks were bright pink as she slipped out of bed and skittered to her trunk, throwing open the lid. She paused, dissolving into a laugh and shaking her head. "All right, it is that." She straightened and dragged her eyes over to meet his.

Of course, that was the exact moment that the towel chose to fall off as he reached for his britches on the far end of the bureau. He fumbled for the towel and missed. It plopped to the floor as he pivoted in such a way that exposed more than he intended to. Elspeth gasped and slapped a hand to her mouth…but only to hide a giddy giggle. She spun away, her shoulders still shaking with mirth. If Athos wasn't mistaken, there was a certain sparkle in her eyes.

"Sorry, sorry," he laughed, scrambling to pick up the towel and retrieve his britches and a pair of trousers to boot.

Although if he wasn't mistaken, a certain long-ignored part of him leapt to life, more sensitive and reactive than it had been in years. He blushed furiously and turned away, getting dressed as fast as he could, casting a scolding look and pointing a stern finger of warning at his wayward organ.

He waited until he was fully dressed in his uniform before risking a glance at Elspeth. The beautiful and soft-spoken woman had set to work making their bed rather than attempting to bathe or change in front of him. It was another mark in her favor.

"I'll just go downstairs and start breakfast," he said, rushing toward the door. "Although I think I hear Ivy and Heather down there already."

"You can tell it's them?" She turned to him, brow lifted.

"Yes. It must be Ivy and Heather, since Piper isn't here. They're trying to be quiet, there are no crashes of dropped pots, and since they're twins and have a way of communicating without words—unlike the boys, who aren't twins—I don't hear any whispering."

Elspeth smiled. "Clever. And I'm sorry, I should have gotten up earlier to make breakfast myself."

"No, no." Athos waved away her apology as he opened the bedroom door and took one step into the hall. "You were exhausted last night and needed sleep. We'll ease you into motherhood." He risked winking at her—good grief, he hadn't winked at anyone in years—and zipped out into the hall.

He was right about Ivy and Heather starting breakfast. As he walked into the kitchen, the smell of bacon frying filled the air. He breathed it in with a happy sigh and went to kiss each of his girls on the cheek. As they minded the bacon and began frying eggs, he did his best to tidy up. Tidying was a hopeless operation, though. Perhaps if he had an extra set of hands, like the strange drawing of a Hindu god that he'd once seen.

"I'm so sorry that I wasn't here to help you with

breakfast." Minutes later, Elspeth was apologizing before she was fully in the kitchen.

"That's all right."

"We don't mind."

Athos grinned at the grace and responsibility of the twins. How he managed to raise such polite and helpful children was beyond him. Natalie had had a hand in Ivy and Heather's childhood, even though she'd been gone for over four years now. That had to explain it. That also probably explained why the house erupted into noise as soon as the younger children were awake.

"Bacon, bacon, bacon!" Thomas's shout could be heard all through the upstairs hall and down the stairs as he charged into the kitchen.

"I can't find my stockings," Geneva called a few minutes later.

"Papa! Hubert is hogging the wash water," Lael hollered not long after that.

The sunny calm of morning was broken. The day's battles had begun. Footsteps clunked and thumped around the house, bacon sizzled, pots rattled, and plates clinked as the whirlwind of breakfast got underway. Athos watched as Elspeth went from smiling to concentrating with all her might to wide-eyed panic as she tried to keep up.

"I'm sorry about all the chaos," he apologized as they all sat down to gobble down the meal before the older kids had to rush off to school. "You'll—"

"—get used to it." Elspeth finished his sentence with a smile. "I'm sure I will."

"Papa, do you have to go to work today?" Millicent asked from Elspeth's end of the table.

"Yes, sweetheart," Athos answered, heart squeezing. "There's an early train today, and I have to be there to unload it. And then there's another train coming from the west this afternoon."

"I hate trains," Geneva sighed.

"You should take a day off, since you got married yesterday," Hubert said with a philosophic tilt of his head.

"Yeah, and we shouldn't have to go to school today," Vernon added. "We need to get to know our new mother better, after all."

Athos laughed. "Nice try, my boy."

The others giggled, then proceeded to make their own arguments about why they should stay home from school. It was all in fun, but in the process of debating and laughing and coming up with ideas of things they could do instead of school that would be equally as educational, the hands of the clock moved a little too much.

"We're late," Heather cried out all at once. "We're late for school!"

Another rush of chaos followed as the children all jumped up from the table and scrambled to find their books and shoes. The older kids were quicker and managed to get out the door fast enough, but Lael, Geneva, and Millicent lagged behind.

"Come on," Athos encouraged them, tossing an apologetic smile Elspeth's way as they crouched before the tardy ones, tying shoes and fixing hair bows. "You're going to make me late too."

As if to emphasize the point, a train whistle blew in the distance. All joking was over, and Athos joined the rush. The three kids managed to make it out the door as he hurried back upstairs to grab his uniform jacket, then thundered downstairs and into the kitchen, where Elspeth had begun to clean up.

"Geneva, Millie, and Lael only have a half day of school today since it's Friday," he rushed to inform her.

"They'll be home for lunch around noon. The older ones will be back by three. Fridays are usually laundry days. If you need anything, Josephine Evans is right next door and can help a bit."

"All right." Elspeth nodded, a little out of breath.

Athos searched for his hat, found it sitting inside the breadbox, reached for it and settled it on his head, along with a shower of crumbs. "If things get really dicey, send Hubert down to the station to fetch me. He's not supposed to work today. I told him he'd be a much bigger help at home until you're settled."

"Right."

"Papa, Papa!" Thomas shot into the room from the hall, smashing into Athos's legs and hugging him. "Goodbye, goodbye, goodbye!"

"Be nice for Elspeth now." He bent over to hug Thomas. As soon as he let the boy go, he turned and gave Elspeth a quick peck on the cheek out of long-forgotten habit, the way he always had with Natalie.

Both Athos and Elspeth widened their eyes and stiffened in surprise. For a long moment, their eyes met. Something warm and tender shifted in Athos's heart. He found himself wanting to give her another, longer kiss, and not on the cheek.

"Well." He cleared his throat and started for the door. "I really do need to get going. Busy day ahead!"

Busy enough that his heart was still racing as he rushed out the door and hurried to the station.

Work was not something young women of Elspeth's social class were supposed to do, and yet, as she bent over the Strong family's enormous washtub in the downstairs washroom, scrubbing dresses and knickers, shirts and underclothes in all sizes imaginable, Elspeth considered that she was quite good at it. At least for someone who hadn't worked a day in her life before her nineteenth birthday.

Working and minding children at the same time, however, was another thing.

"Bleh!" Thomas exclaimed with sudden violence from his place in the hall just on the other side of the washroom doorway.

Elspeth glanced up to see him making a horrible face, his tongue stuck out and covered with white flakes. "Oh, Thomas, no, no!" She pulled back from the washtub with a splash, rushing to yank a box of laundry soap out of the young boy's hands.

"It looks like mashed potatoes," he complained, tongue still hanging out. "It hurts!"

Elspeth didn't need to look at the box's label to know there was lye in the soap flakes. She rushed Thomas to the kitchen and rinsed his mouth with copious amounts of water, urging him not to swallow the whole time. There were a few tears, but with a thorough rinse and a glass of milk—which Elspeth had once heard could help if someone swallowed soap, but had no idea whether it was actually true—Thomas was none the worse for wear.

"I nearly died!" Thomas announced to Geneva, Millicent, and Lael when the younger children came home at lunchtime.

"You did not nearly die." Elspeth laughed, her smile tight, trying to reassure the children as much as herself.

"Wow!" Lael exclaimed, helping himself to the plate of leftover chicken and vegetables that Elspeth had prepared for them. "I wish *I* had almost died."

"Believe me, you don't," Elspeth told him.

"I bet if I climbed really high in the tree outside then jumped, I might almost die too!"

"Oh good gracious, Lael." Elspeth pressed a hand to her heart. "Please don't try it."

Their cozy meal was interrupted by a knock at the door. "Hello?"

"It's Mrs. Murphy," Millicent explained. She jumped up from her seat at the kitchen table and tore through the house to greet the newly arrived neighbor.

Mrs. Katie Murphy turned out to be one of Elspeth's nearest neighbors. She was a charming Irishwoman in her middle years who had been among the first to journey out to Haskell eleven years ago, when the town was founded. But as much as Elspeth enjoyed being introduced to the woman and chatting for a few minutes, the laundry was still overflowing, the breakfast dishes hadn't been cleared from the dining room table, and the four youngest Strong children were growing louder and louder in the kitchen as they finished their lunch and began playing their favorite game: train wreck.

"Perhaps I'll come back another day and we can get to know each other better," Mrs. Murphy laughed after Elspeth glanced over her shoulder for the thousandth time to see what the children were up to. She departed with a kind farewell.

"I like Mrs. Murphy," Geneva informed Elspeth as she returned to the kitchen to make sure the kids were finished eating. "She has red hair. And Morgan Murphy is in mine and Millie's class in school. He has red hair too."

"You shall have to invite them over to play sometime," Elspeth said, breathless and distracted as she put away the remaining food.

"Yes, I shall." Geneva imitated her accent, but it was clear to Elspeth that in this case the imitation was intended to be flattery.

She didn't have much time to think of it either way. As soon as the children were fed and their hands and faces washed, she lugged the huge, heavy basket of clean laundry out to the backyard and began hanging it up to dry.

"Can I climb the tree?" Lael asked before she had two shirts hung. He eyed the tree with longing and mischief.

"Not if you intend to throw yourself to your almost death," Elspeth answered.

"You climb up the tree and we'll throw rocks at you," Millicent suggested.

"Yes! Yes!"

"Girls, I hardly think—" Elspeth began.

But Lael was quick to answer, "Okay!"

"But—"

Lael scrambled up the tree before Elspeth could stop

him. The twins and Thomas ran around the base of the tree, giggling and looking for rocks.

"They do that all the time."

Elspeth straightened from the laundry basket and whipped around to find the older woman who had spoken. "They do?"

The older woman was hanging her own laundry in the yard beside the Strong house. She laughed. "Believe it or not, they do. If you ask me, it's good practice for the girls. They will be fine pitchers on one of Haskell's baseball teams someday." The woman finished fastening a pair of long underwear, wiped her hands on her apron, then crossed the few yards that separated the two laundry lines to shake Elspeth's hand. "Josephine Evans. I don't believe we've been properly introduced yet."

"Oh." Elspeth finished hanging one of the older twins' petticoats, then took her neighbor's hand. "Elspeth Leo—Strong." She smiled as she used her new name for the first time.

"I know." Josephine nodded. "We've all been waiting for Athos to remarry for a long time. Why, he started talking about it last Christmas, before that, even. You'd be hard pressed to find a soul in Haskell who doesn't know Athos or wish him well."

As happy as Elspeth was to hear that Athos's neighbors liked and respected him, the more Josephine talked, the more Elspeth ached to get back to hanging laundry. She didn't suppose clothes could mold in the laundry basket, but the longer it took for her to hang them, the longer it would take for them to dry. And she still had to iron the shirts and dresses once they were dry.

"Yeow!" A loud cry from Lael—halfway up the tree—pulled both Elspeth's and Josephine's attention. "You hit me!"

"But you told us to throw rocks at you," Millicent complained.

"You were supposed to miss."

"Excuse me." Elspeth dismissed herself from her conversation with Josephine, hoping she wasn't being unfriendly, and raced to the bottom of the tree. "If you didn't want to be hit with rocks, you shouldn't have told your sisters to throw them."

"I'm a good rock thrower," Thomas informed her. He promptly attempted to hurl a small, sharp rock, let go at the wrong time, and hurled the rock right into his foot. His bare foot. When had he taken off his shoes?

The question was banished from Elspeth's mind as Thomas broke into a wail. She scooped him into her arms to comfort him, dabbing at the tiny trickle of blood he'd managed to draw with the corner of her apron.

"I want to help hang the laundry," Geneva declared.

"Me too!"

The girls dashed for the basket and the clothesline before Elspeth could think about it.

"I almost died again," Thomas wailed.

"I'm sorry, is this a bad time?"

Elspeth glanced around the corner of the house to find a handsome and very pregnant black woman in an exquisite gown rounding the corner. "Wendy!" She was so surprised to see her old friend from Hurst Home that she stood. In the process, Thomas slipped off her lap, his feet—injured and whole—landing in a puddle made by the wash water.

"Ooh!" He declared, then started stomping. Muddy water flew everywhere.

"It *is* a bad time," Wendy laughed. She waddled around to meet Elspeth on the garden path anyhow, giving her a hug. "I just wanted to say hello and see how you're settling in."

"Well enough, I suppose." As wonderful as it was to see Wendy again, and as much catching up as she longed to do, the laundry still needed to be hung, and now Thomas was covered from head to toe in muddy water.

"Travis and I live on the other side of the yard there." Wendy pointed through a hedge at the back of the Strong property to the backyard of another building. "I can see you're busy right now, but I wanted to invite you to tea at some point.

"I'd love to come." Elspeth brushed splatters of mud off of her apron. feeling decidedly feeble compared to her stately friend. "I just don't know when I'll possibly have time."

"The Strong children are a handful, aren't they? I hope mine and Travis's little bundle of joy has just as much energy." Wendy patted her stomach, then proceeded to go on and talk all about how delightful the Strong children were and how she and Travis hoped to have many of their own. Time itched down Elspeth's back like prickles of fire. Lael continued to climb around in the tree nearly directly above them.

It wasn't until Vernon's call of, "We're home," followed by the older four children pouring out onto the back porch from the kitchen that Elspeth dared to drag her polite attention away from Wendy to see what was going on. What she found was Geneva and Millicent hanging dirt and grass stained clothes on the line.

"Oh no!" She left Wendy and rushed to the clothesline.

"Do you need me to help with that?" Wendy offered. She started to waddle forward, one hand on her back.

Elspeth couldn't let a very pregnant woman stoop and reach and otherwise strain herself over a little bit of spoiled laundry. "No, you should be at home resting." She tried to sound lighthearted but was afraid she was more of a shrew.

"We'll help," Ivy and Heather said in unison.

"What's wrong?" Geneva asked as her sisters joined them.

"We're just hanging laundry," Millie added.

"You've dragged it through the grass and mud," Heather pointed out.

"Oh."

"Do we have any food?" Hubert asked from the porch rail.

Elspeth didn't have time to check to see if Wendy had gone or not. "I'm sure there's something in the pantry," she said, rushing back to the porch.

"I want to climb the tree too," Vernon hollered, rushing for the tree. "Hey Millie, Neva, you wanna throw rocks at me?"

"No!" Elspeth had reached the porch steps as the question was asked. She whirled back, intent on stopping the mischief, but it was too late. Geneva and Millicent were racing back to the tree.

Elspeth only barely noticed the older lady in a grey suit, her hair pulled back under a small, black hat, a large, flat purse of some sort clutched in her hands. She wore a brittle smile that was fading fast as she glanced around the yard, taking in each set of children in turn.

"Look at me," Thomas yelled, holding out his arms. "I'm covered in mud and I nearly died twice today!"

The grey suit lady's eyes went wide, and her lips pursed in a disapproving line.

"How did you nearly die?" Hubert asked, moving to

lean against the porch railing above where Elspeth and Thomas stood.

"I ate soap," Thomas declared proudly.

Hubert laughed. "I'm so hungry I could eat soap. I haven't eaten in ages."

A sudden shout of alarm came from the tree above along with a heavy rustling and a flash of downward movement. Geneva and Millicent screamed. Even Vernon cried out in wordless fright. A moment later, the movement stopped with a rustle.

"It's okay," Lael announced, a little tremulously. "I fell off a branch, but I caught the next one down." He tried to laugh. "Nearly dying isn't as much fun as I thought it would be."

Elspeth's mouth opened as she tried to think of the right way to scold the boy into next Sunday.

"Excuse me," the grey suit woman said. No one paid her any mind at first, so she barked, "*Excuse me!*"

Elspeth fought not to roll her eyes. "I'm sorry." She left Thomas where he was in the mud puddle and marched around to the woman, not even trying to be polite now. "I'm sorry, but I've had quite enough visits from neighbors for one day. I would be delighted to meet you some other time, but as you can see, I have my hands full."

The grey suit woman's nostrils flared, and splotches of red began to form on her face. "I am *not* a neighbor," she said in clipped tones.

Elspeth blinked. "I'm not buying anything," she said, far less friendly. "I'm not even sure peddling is legal in this town."

"Well!" the woman exclaimed in sharp offense. "I am not selling anything."

"Then please leave." Every last bit of politeness was gone from Elspeth's tone.

The woman's face hardened. Her already square jaw grew sharp and her eyes narrowed. "Are you the mother of these children?"

Elspeth was too exhausted to explain. Lael had climbed down from the tree, and the youngest four were running like a bear was chasing them through the yard. Vernon was throwing something down from the tree onto Ivy and Heather as they worked, provoking shouts of protest.

"I'm Mrs. Strong," Elspeth answered.

A tight, smug grin spread across the woman's face. She reached into her flat bag and took out a formal-looking paper. "I'm Mrs. Margaret Lyon from the Society for Prevention of Cruelty to Children." She thrust the paper at Elspeth. "Under order of the government of the Territory of Wyoming, I have been charged with taking these children into custody to prevent any further abuse to their persons or minds."

The bottom dropped out of Elspeth's stomach. She barely managed to hold onto the paper when Mrs. Lyon let go. "What?"

"I'm taking these children into custody," Mrs. Lyon repeated. She turned back to the front part of the yard and gestured. Four large, burly men came forward from the picket fence that separated the front yard from the street. "Round them up," she ordered.

"Yes, ma'am."

Elspeth scrambled to look at the paper she'd been handed. She knew nothing—absolutely nothing—about societies for the prevention of cruelty to anything or laws in Wyoming. The document looked zealously complicated and legal as she scanned over it. The only things that really stood out were the words "Order for immediate removal from negligent parent" and "As reported by Mr. Rex Bonneville." The name rang a bell, but Elspeth couldn't put a face to it.

"You can't do this," she insisted, staring Mrs. Lyon down.

"The judge signed there." Mrs. Lyon leaned over to point out a squiggly signature, her smile so self-satisfied that Elspeth had to fight the urge to punch the woman in the face.

"No!" Thomas was the first one to scream in terror, but right away, Geneva and Millicent joined him.

Elspeth whipped around to find three of the four strong-arms chasing after the younger children. One scooped Thomas up without trouble, but Geneva, Millie, Lael, and Vernon were giving the others a vicious chase. The fourth thug had Hubert, Ivy, and Heather cornered on the stairs. Hubert's fists were balled and he looked like he would overcome the shock that painted his face and start fighting any second.

"Leave them alone," Elspeth shouted, rushing into the heart of the fray.

"Elspeth, Elspeth!" Thomas cried for her, stretching out his arms even as the tough that held him clamped harder around his waist.

Millicent ran right at Elspeth and slammed into her, grabbing her waist for dear life, panting and whimpering, as Geneva was swept up by one of the other men.

"You leave my sister alone!" Hubert snapped at last, surging forward. He was stopped when the man guarding him and the older twins thrust out an arm to keep him on the stairs. Hubert ran right into that arm, and the result looked a little too much like the man had punched him in the stomach.

Elspeth screamed in wordless outrage, but with Millie clinging to her, she couldn't move.

"The Society for Prevention of Cruelty to Children has made it our crusade to stop the heartless abuse and neglect of our most precious resource, our children." Mrs. Lyon spoke in supercilious tones, her nose in the air, as the children continued to scream and wail. She could have been addressing a room full of lawyers for all the emotion she showed. "From the factory floor to the unfit home, we have made it our mission to rescue children in dire circumstances from the degradation of unfit parenting."

"You call this a *rescue*?" Elspeth snapped in outrage.

Lael let out a ferocious howl as he was caught and lugged back to the stairs. The men who had caught Geneva and Thomas handed them off to the stair guard, then went after Vernon together. Vernon had climbed the tree and was shouting for help at the top of his lungs.

"No child shall be oppressed while our vigilant eyes oversee them," Mrs. Lyon went on, her smile turning almost rapturous as she spouted her drivel. "We are angels of mercy, intent on God's work, and we shall bring these poor, neglected souls to a gentler understanding of life and morality."

"You're taking them from their father," Elspeth shouted. "Their father loves them."

"Love is not dirt and drudgery." Mrs. Lyon sniffed. "Why look at the state of that one." She tossed a gesture at Thomas and turned up her nose.

"I nearly died three times today," Thomas wailed.

Elspeth cringed, but that was all she could do.

The thugs chasing Vernon began to shake the tree he'd climbed. For all his twelve years, Vernon still cried out in fear. "I'll come down, I'll come down," he vowed, sobbing.

"You're frightening them," Elspeth yelled. "You call that a mission of mercy?"

"Sometimes the initial extraction can appear to be painful." Mrs. Lyon glanced at her fingernails, turning her hand this way and that, and sniffing as if the wailing around her was of no consequence. "They'll be so much happier once they've undergone our strict program of moral and physical education."

"*What*?"

Before Elspeth's question could be answered, Vernon dropped out of the tree and into the arms of one of the thugs. The other marched over to her and ripped Millicent away. Millie screamed, Vernon was sobbing in fear and shame, and the rest of the children were weeping bitterly. Except Hubert, who looked as though he might commit murder any second.

"Hold on, children." Elspeth rushed over to where they had all been gathered on the stairs. Two of the thugs rounded on her, holding out their arms to keep her away. She ignored them. "Hold on. This is a mistake. Just a horrible mistake. Please be patient and obedient for now."

No sooner were the words out of her mouth then Mrs. Lyon called, "Bring them along."

The four thugs lifted, pushed, and herded the children off the stairs and around the yard toward the front of the house.

"What? Wait! Where are you taking them?" Elspeth rushed after them. She spotted Josephine and a girl about Hubert's age running out of their house. A small crowd waited around the front in the street.

"The paper explains it all," Mrs. Lyon said, full of disdain. "The children are being removed from their abusive parent. Removed means taken away," she added as if Elspeth were stupid as well as negligent.

"But where are you taking them?" Elspeth demanded over the cries and protests of the children.

"To the hotel."

For whatever reason, that announcement lessened the children's shrieks and panic.

"I have engaged a suite at the hotel where the children will be kept until such a time as a place can be made for them at the Cheyenne Home for Miscreant Children."

"There is no such thing," Hubert shouted.

"There is," Mrs. Lyon replied ominously.

Elspeth's mind reeled. She glanced at the paper in her hands once more, but the words didn't make any more sense this time than they had before. She jogged to keep up with the cluster as they marched toward the large, white hotel Athos had pointed out to her the day before. Mrs. Lyon walked with her nose on the air, a superior, oblivious smile on her face. Elspeth still wanted to slap the woman, but that wasn't going to help. No, the only thing she could think of that would help was Athos.

"Children, be good." She picked up her pace to get as close to the children as the thugs would let her. "This must be some sort of misunderstanding. Stay calm and quiet, and I'll fetch your father."

"Papa, Papa!" The younger ones wailed.

"I'll get him," Elspeth vowed. "And then we'll sort this muddle out."

Chapter Five

Busy days meant better days. The old adage that his mother used to recite when Athos was a boy came back to him now as he worked stacking crates of supplies for the general store that had come in on the second train of the day. The first train had contained more passengers than cargo, including the curious group consisting of one woman in a tight, grey suit and four men that would have been more in their element in a logging camp than escorting one woman. Athos didn't think much of it, though.

No, if he was going to think about any woman, it was going to be his new wife. Charlie Garrett and the others involved with the women at Hurst Home had hit a homerun with Elspeth, as far as he was concerned. He grinned like a fool as he loaded crates for the general store into Lex Kline's wagon. Elspeth was intelligent and capable, and darn near the prettiest woman he'd seen in ages. He'd had a hard time not staring at her hair—dark and rich as chocolate—when she'd taken it down before bed the night before. He'd had a hard time not staring at other things about her too. A nightgown could only conceal so much. Then again, she'd gotten an eyeful of more of him than he'd bargained for that morning.

"That's the smile of a man content with his lot."

Athos turned to find Gideon Faraday approaching him from the other end of the platform. He laughed as he hoisted the last crate into Lex's wagon. "I'm feeling remarkably content with my lot in life this morning."

Gideon thumped him on the back as soon as he was close enough. "I can't wait to meet your new wife. Whispers already say she's something special."

"You know, I think she is." Athos didn't mean to sound so mystified as he spoke, but the fact that such a wonderful woman could have been paired with him was baffling as far as he was concerned.

"I hear she's English," Gideon went on.

Athos blinked. "Yes, I think she is." He laughed. "Of course she is. I don't know why I didn't ask her about that yesterday."

"Love makes us forget everything," Gideon said.

"Oh, it's not love," Athos insisted. "We've only just met, after all. And I wouldn't ask someone like Elspeth for something so…so personal. Not until we've known each other for years at least. And even then we'll probably be too busy to feel anything at all." Like he and Natalie had been. The thought was disquieting, so he cleared his throat and shook it off.

He rapped on the back of Lex's wagon to let the man know the loading was finished, then turned and headed up onto the platform with Gideon.

"What can I do for you today, Gid?" he asked.

"I'm just checking to see if the equipment I ordered came in." Gideon followed him into the warehouse portion of the stationhouse.

"This last train had dozens of boxes on it," he said, searching through the piles he'd made earlier. "I had to get the train porters to help me unload, and they weren't happy about that. I told them it was either that or make the train late."

"Have you considered asking Howard to pay for an assistant?" Gideon asked.

The question went unanswered. Before Athos could so much as open his mouth, he was startled by Elspeth's cry of, "Athos! Athos!"

Dropping everything, Athos dashed out of the stationhouse. He searched the platform, then rushed around the side, only to see Elspeth tearing down Main Street toward him. His heart shot to his throat. Was someone injured? Was the house on fire? Had one of his children caused a riot?

"Athos!" Elspeth skidded to a breathless halt near the edge of the platform.

Athos leapt down to catch her. "What? What is it? Are the children hurt?"

She shook her head, face pinched, eyes red-rimmed and glassy, then gulped for air. "They've been taken."

"What?" He tightened his hold on Elspeth's arms. His heart thundered in his chest. He hugged Elspeth close on instinct. "What happened?"

She struggled away from him enough to hand him a piece of crumpled parchment. "A Mrs. Margaret Lyon from the Society for Prevention of Cruelty to Children claimed that they were being mistreated. She had four men with her. They snatched up the children and took them away to the hotel."

"No!" Panic washed through Athos in a nauseating wave. His hands shook as he stared at the parchment, trying to make sense of what was printed on it. He'd seen his fair share of legal documents as stationmaster, but this was outrageous.

At least, it was outrageous until he noticed a key piece of information near the bottom: by the order of Rex Bonneville.

"Bonneville," he growled, fury taking over from fear.

"Who?"

"Rex Bonneville." He balled his hand into a fist around the parchment. "There was an incident a few weeks ago, before you came," he explained quickly, pivoting and marching up onto the platform, Elspeth by his side. "Lael, Neva, Millie, and Thomas bumped into Bonneville's daughters after church, causing a spill and knocking a table of food onto them. There have been other instances where the kids have upset the Bonneville sisters as well, but that one…" He sighed, some of his energy leaving him as the reality of the situation grabbed hold of him. "Rex said I would regret this."

"That's awful," Elspeth exclaimed. "What kind of man would order children taken from their father as an act of revenge?"

"Rex Bonneville," Athos answered.

They crossed into the station office, where Athos grabbed his uniform jacket. He shrugged into it as they headed out again. No one took his children and got away with it.

"What's this I hear about Bonneville causing trouble with the children?" Gideon—who was still looking for his shipment in the warehouse room—asked as they marched past.

Athos was too outraged to answer the question. "Gideon, would you be able to mind the station while I deal with this?"

"Absolutely," Gideon answered without hesitation. "I'll help in any way I can."

"Thanks."

Athos continued around the edge of the platform and out into the street. He grabbed Elspeth's hand when they started up Main Street, fearing that he would need her courage—and possibly her restraint—to deal with this.

"That woman took the children to the hotel," Elspeth told him as they half walked, half ran.

"The hotel?" Athos skipped a step, then doubled his speed.

"She said she rented a suite there."

His panic eased by a hair. Everyone knew The Cattleman Hotel was neutral territory in Haskell. More than that, it was overseen by Theophilus Gunn, one of the few people Athos could trust in a situation like this.

Indeed, as Athos and Elspeth rushed up the steps of the hotel's porch and barged through the front door into the lobby, Gunn was standing near the front desk, as though he was expecting them.

But Gunn wasn't the only one. Rex Bonneville and all four of his daughters loitered suspiciously in the lobby as well, as if waiting for a baseball game to begin. Athos didn't know which direction to run in or which demands to make first.

A sharp cry of "Papa!" from the hallway to the right of the front desk decided him.

"Millie!" He dropped Elspeth's hand and darted for the side hall just as someone grabbed Millie and yanked her away.

Millie's sharp scream was followed by excited and frightened shouts from all of his children. Athos made it around the corner and into the hall just as a door slammed shut at the far end. The shouts and pleas of his children continued on the other side as two muscular men—two of the ones he had seen getting off the train—stood guard in front of it. The woman in the grey suit that he had seen earlier was just straightening from the door, a hotel key in her hand. She turned to Athos with a frigid smile.

"What is the meaning of this?" Athos demanded, charging down the hall. "By whose authority have you kidnapped my children?"

The cries of "Papa, Papa!" on the other side of the door abruptly stopped, and Athos had the feeling his children were listening. They weren't the only ones. The lobby end of the hall quickly filled with Bonnevilles, Elspeth, and Gunn.

The woman in the grey suit stepped away from the door, her back straight, her nose tilted up in disgust, and advanced toward him. "I suppose you are the *father*." She said the word as though saying he was the drunkard. She must have been the Mrs. Lyon Elspeth mentioned earlier.

"Yes." Athos moved to stand toe-to-toe with her, shoulders squared, jaw set. "Give me my children back."

Mrs. Lyon cleared her throat and picked an imaginary piece of lint from her sleeve. Without looking at him, she said, "I see you have the court order in your hand. You have been deemed an unfit parent, and I, as representative of the Society for Prevention of Cruelty to Children, have performed the necessary act of *mercy* in removing the mistreated children from your home."

"My children are not mistreated," Athos boomed. "They are loved and cared for."

Behind the door, cries of, "We are!" "Papa loves us!" "He's the best papa in the world!" rang out.

A muffled voice within the room shouted at the children to be quiet. The supportive shouts instantly stopped. Athos saw red.

"You will let my children out of that room at once," he demanded. "You have no right to keep them prisoner."

"This is a hotel, not a prison," Mrs. Lyon sniffed. "And they are only being secured in this room to prevent you from doing them further harm."

"*Further harm*?" Athos bellowed in outrage. He might have been a fool, but he wasn't so big of a fool that he couldn't see dealing with Mrs. Lyon was pointless. He whipped around, marching back down the hall toward Rex Bonneville. "You're behind this."

Bonneville crossed his arms and stood straighter. "I don't deny it. The way those children behave is a disgrace."

"It's about time someone put a stop to it." Vivian echoed her father's pose, crossing her arms and tilting her chin up to look down her nose at Athos.

"Yes, and that someone is us," Bebe added, trying but failing to have the same authority as her father and oldest sister.

"This is going too far." Athos wasn't about to be intimidated by Bonneville. "These are my children. They are my life. You can't just take them away from me."

"A court in Cheyenne says I can." Bonneville shrugged. "I presented ample evidence to the territory office for housing and citizenry."

"What does that have to do with anything?" Elspeth interjected. "I've never even heard of it."

The Bonneville sisters stared at Elspeth, raking her with glances from the top of her head to the bottom of her feet.

"Who are you?" Melinda asked.

"I'm Mrs. Athos Strong," she told them, planting her hands on her hips.

A sudden burst of pride and relief that Elspeth was

on his side filled Athos. "I sent for her from Hurst Home and we were married yesterday." He rounded on Bonneville. "Elspeth is here to help care for the children."

"Clearly she's not up to the task," Mrs. Lyon interrupted. "When I went to the house to rescue the children it was in a deplorable state. Laundry was scattered all over the backyard. The two oldest girls were engaged in slave labor hanging it on the line."

"What?" Elspeth barked in protest. "They had kindly offered to help."

"Two of the boys were stranded in a tree where one nearly fell to his death," Mrs. Lyon went on. "The younger ones were screaming like banshees. The oldest implied that he hadn't been fed for days."

"Hubert is a growing boy. He's always hungry," Athos protested.

Mrs. Lyon ignored him. "And the youngest admitted that he had nearly died twice that day, once by consuming soap."

"They're children," Athos roared. "They're lively, curious, industrious *children*."

"They are in harm's way and they have been removed," Mrs. Lyon insisted.

"I want them back." Athos moved as if to rush down the hall. Mrs. Lyon stepped into his path, and the two men guarding the door rushed forward to protect her.

"You had your chance, Strong," Bonneville said, a sly grin narrowing his eyes. "You are a failure as a father. The law and the government of this great territory has finally caught up with you."

Athos wheeled back to face down Bonneville. "You mean your crony friends in the Wyoming Stock Grower's Association stepped in to do your dirty work. Everyone knows that little club controls the territorial government."

Bonneville shrugged, not denying it. "Either way, your children will be placed in foster homes as the Society for Prevention of Cruelty to Children sees fit. Even if they have to be split up," he added with a vicious smirk.

"No, you can't," Elspeth gasped.

"What do you care?" Vivian snapped.

"You barely know them," Melinda added.

"Yeah, you just got here yesterday," Bebe finished.

"Perhaps we should give them a chance to explain," Honoria added, inching sideways to come out of the shadows where she'd hidden. Her eyes were rimmed with shadows, and she coughed before going on with, "Mr. Strong has remarried, after all. Maybe all the children need is a new mother to help settle them."

"Shut up, Honoria," Vivian snapped.

"These children obviously need to be sent to reform school," Melinda added.

"That or the workhouse," Bebe said. She paused and frowned. "Does America have workhouses or will we have to ship them to England for that?"

"No one is being sent to the workhouse," Gunn stepped in, holding up his hands to quiet both sides. "The children are safe in the hotel until we sort this confusion out."

"There's nothing to sort out," Mrs. Lyon insisted. "I have a court order for their removal."

"Let me see."

Athos quickly handed over the crumpled parchment. Gunn studied it with a frown. As he did, Athos shifted closer to Elspeth. He might feel a bit calmer if he held her hand. But Elspeth was busy staring intently at Gunn.

"This order contains a clause allowing Athos to appeal the decision," Gunn announced.

"What?" Mrs. Lyon, Bonneville, and his daughters barked at the same time.

"It says right here that Athos has the right to ask for an impartial judge to hear the case and make a decision of appeal." Gunn lowered the document. "I suggest we wire for a judge to come to Haskell immediately."

"Theophilus Gunn!" Elspeth's exclamation was so sudden and so out of tune with the scene that more than just Athos started. "I didn't make the connection before."

"Do you know him?" Athos asked.

Elspeth sent him a quick glance before turning back to Gunn with a wide smile. "I...I think I used to." She blinked and took a step closer, studying Gunn as though reading a forgotten favorite book. "My uncle Stephen once had a valet named Theophilus Gunn. Uncle Stephen was killed in the Crimea, but our family has kept in touch with the valet. Mr. Gunn used to visit when I was just a girl. Is it really you?"

Gunn's eyes widened as he studied Elspeth right back. He then broke into a wide smile. "Lady Elspeth! You're so grown up that I didn't recognize you." He stepped forward and took her hand, bending over to kiss her knuckles like a man approaching a queen. "It's a pleasure to see you again, my lady."

"*My lady*?" Vivian Bonneville snapped.

Athos recovered from his own shock long enough to send a glance Vivian's way. The Bonneville sisters had gone from turning up their noses at him and Elspeth to studying Elspeth with a jumble of confusion and fascination. And just a little bit of awe.

"You're a lady?" Melinda asked.

"As in, a real, fancy, honest-to-God lady with a title and everything?" Bebe blurted.

Elspeth turned bright pink as she stepped away from Gunn. Athos caught a flash of cunning in her eyes before she executed a perfect curtsy for the Bonneville sisters. "I'm afraid I am." She raised her eyes with regal steadiness and went on to say, "My father is the Marquis of Southampton."

The Bonneville sisters gasped audibly. They began to blubber and flutter and fall all over themselves to mimic Elspeth's curtsy.

"It's a pleasure to meet you, *my lady*," Melinda said.

"You must come to tea at our house, *my lady*," Vivian agreed.

"Wow! A real lady," Bebe snorted.

Honoria simply smiled and said, "Hello."

Silence followed. Bonneville frowned, his daughtered preened and primped. Athos stood there with his jaw hanging open, not quite sure what had just happened.

"What's going on out there?" Hubert called from behind the door.

"You're too quiet," Heather's voice followed.

That spurred Mrs. Lyon into action. "Enough of this nonsense. The children are in my care, and they will be taken to Cheyenne to be distributed to better homes."

"The children will stay here," Gunn contradicted her, "until a judge can be sent for to hear an appeal to the case."

"Right." Athos nodded, then withered. "Are you certain they have to stay here? They're my children, they should come home."

Gunn moved so that he could rest a hand on Athos's shoulders. "Think of it as giving the children an exciting vacation. Or think of it as a wedding present." The glanced to Elspeth with a smile. "You've just been married and you need some time to get to know your new wife.

Leave the children in my care and take a few days to yourself."

"But…"

Gunn leaned closer. "I'll set the wheels in motion and send for a judge to hear the appeal. In the meantime, I suggest you consult with Solomon."

"Solomon?" Athos blinked in surprise.

"Yes." Gunn nodded, pivoting to explain to Elspeth, "Solomon Templesmith is our town banker, but before he took up finance, he studied the law. He was prevented from practicing back East because of his race, but he still knows the law better than anyone in Haskell."

"Ha," Bonneville sniffed. "If you want to employ that jumped-up darkie to fight your case for you, go right ahead. I won't stop you. Come on, girls." He stepped away from the scene, retreating across the lobby and toward the door.

As the Bonnevilles moved away from the end of the hall, it became apparent that several other hotel guests had flooded the lobby to see what was going on. Now that the excitement was over, they rushed to look as innocent as possible.

Mrs. Lyon cleared her throat, face scrunched as though she'd eaten something sour. "If I'm going to be forced to stay here until a judge can confirm the opinion of the Society for Prevention of Cruelty to Children, then I expect to be fed and sheltered appropriately."

"Of course." Gunn inclined his head to the woman, but his expression had gone so stony that Athos had no doubt Gunn wasn't happy.

"And someone must send bundles of the children's clothing to the hotel at once," Mrs. Lyon went on.

"Of course. I'll see to it," Elspeth said.

"Not you." Mrs. Lyon sneered. "Someone *reliable* and uninvolved with this deplorable man."

Anger poured through Athos all over again. "Elspeth is perfectly capable of—"

"I'll see if Mrs. Evans next door can do it." Elspeth put a hand on Athos's arm to calm him.

"That sounds like a good idea," Gunn agreed. "Until then, I'll keep an eye on things here. The best you can do right now is to head home."

That *was* the best thing he could do, but it didn't put Athos any more at ease. In fact, now that the surge of action was over, he was left feeling cold and hollow. He turned to glance over his shoulder at the door and the men guarding it. His heart twisted in his chest.

"Don't you worry, kids," he called out. "Your Papa is going to get to the bottom of this."

"Good luck, Papa!"

"You can do it!"

"I love you!"

The calls that came from the other side of the door broke Athos's heart as much as they strengthened it. He was close to unmanning himself with tears as Elspeth took his arm and led him out of the hotel.

Chapter Six

Stunned by the afternoon's events and how quickly a family's fortunes could change, Elspeth walked with Athos out of the hotel, around the corner, and home. Guilt gnawed at her. One day. Not even that. She hadn't completed a single day of being mother to Athos's brood, and the whole lot of them had been taken away. History books would record that she was the most unsuccessful mother in history.

Her thoughts were interrupted by Athos's declaration of, "It's all my fault."

"No, no it isn't," Elspeth insisted, surprised that they had been thinking more or less the same thing, taking on the same burden of responsibility.

"It is." Athos plodded up the stairs and onto his porch.

A battalion of tin soldiers were scattered in one corner, an interrupted doll tea party in another. A few of the downstairs windows had been left open, and sheer curtains billowed out over piles of books one of the older children had left on the windowsill. Silence and the creaking of the boards as Athos crossed to hold the front door open for Elspeth betrayed that even the house was mourning the loss of the children.

"You can't blame yourself," Elspeth insisted, laying a hand on his arm once he came inside, shutting the door behind him.

"I should have spent more time at home," he contradicted her. "I should have remarried sooner or hired someone to help Piper watch the children in the afternoons."

Elspeth shook her head. "It seems to me that you did the best you could, and that those horrible Bonnevilles are to blame."

Athos rubbed a hand over his face, now showing signs of stress and fatigue. "Bonneville is a bully. And I'd say a thing or two about his daughters, but I was told never to speak harshly about a woman." He paused, then said, "Honoria is all right. I don't like watching the way her sisters treat her."

"She was the one with the cough?"

Athos nodded. Then he grimaced. "I don't care what Gunn says about taking care of them while they're at the hotel and treating it like a vacation. My children belong here, in this house, with me."

He finished his declaration, and the two of them stood still. Elspeth lifted her eyes and glanced slowly around. The house seemed bigger somehow, hollow. The breakfast dishes still hadn't been cleared from the table in the dining room to her right. Across the hall in the parlor on the left, the furniture had been moved to create some kind of fort, the books on the shelves had been shoved in willy-nilly, and it appeared as though someone's doll's washing day had resulted in an explosion that took up a corner of the room. Even the hall bore marks of the children, from the pile of shoes caked with dried mud near the front door to the hobby-horse propped up in an alcove.

Through it all, the house was dead quiet, holding its breath.

"I can't take it," Athos said at last, crossing behind Elspeth and heading for the stairs. "I have to do something. I'm going to pack the children's clothes."

"Some of them are still hanging on the wash line out back." Elspeth launched into motion too, heading down the hall, through the kitchen and out to the yard where she'd left her day's work.

Someone had slipped into the backyard and hung the rest of the family's clothes while they had been gone. That was the first thing Elspeth noticed. More than that, the items of clothing that she had sworn the girls had gotten so dirty they would need to be scrubbed again were clean and blowing on the line with the rest of the laundry. The basket had been returned to the porch, along with armfuls of toys that had been scattered throughout the garden. A warm knot filled Elspeth's heart as she walked slowly down the back porch stairs. The only thing left for her to do was to check the chicken coop for eggs and take them inside.

Once in the kitchen, she kept herself in motion by cleaning up from the day's meals. It was both easy and hard to get everything organized, to stack the dishes and put away a few food items that had been left out. Without children under her feet she was able to think and plan. Without children everything around her seemed pale and lifeless.

"These will have to do." Athos shuffled into the kitchen half an hour later with two carpetbags in his hands and one tucked under his arm. His eyes were red-rimmed and puffy, and the very air around him seemed to sag with sadness. "I'll just take them over to Josephine and explain the situation."

He moved on and was out the back door before Elspeth could say anything, before she could question his appearance or throw her arms around him and hug him until they both felt better. The impulse do to just that took her by surprise, yet at the same time it felt perfectly right. She continued with her supper preparations, sniffling and wiping the back of her hand under her eyes.

By the time Athos returned, supper was more than halfway done. Elspeth had prepared the simplest meal she could think of: stew that was made from the remains of the chicken they'd had for supper the night before and whatever vegetables she had been able to find in the pantry.

"We…we need to go shopping," she murmured softly as Athos shuffled to the kitchen table, pulled out a chair, and sat.

"Hmm." He sat with his shoulders slumped, his hands resting on the table. His gaze was unfocused.

"I suppose I could find some time to do the shopping after we speak to Mr.…was it Mr. Templesmith?"

"Yes." Athos shook himself and focused on her. "Solomon Templesmith. He's a good friend of mine. If Gunn has faith in him, then he's who I want to talk to."

Elspeth replied with a hesitant smile. She wasn't sure what else she could do. She turned back to the stove, stirring her stew and wishing there was something more substantial that she could do for her new family.

"So you know Gunn from England, do you?" Athos asked.

"Yes." Elspeth latched onto the topic of conversation, grateful to have something to break the silence. "Like I said, he was my late uncle's valet. They were very close, more like friends than master and servant. I always supposed that was because Mr. Gunn was American and not as steeped in our ways."

"I wonder why Gunn was working as someone's valet in England," Athos said with an exaggerated frown, as if pushing himself to think of something else.

If he was going to use this as a distraction, she would too. "I'm not entirely certain, but I think it had something to do with the army, of all things."

"The army?" He shifted to face her more fully, hanging on her every word.

"Uncle Stephen was a high-ranking officer during the Crimean War. He and Mr. Gunn spent a great deal of time around Sevastopol and the Russian Empire."

"Really?" Athos's interest was genuine instead of strained for a moment.

Elspeth nodded. "When I was a girl, I used to imagine they were spies, stealing secrets for the Queen. But then Uncle Stephen was killed in battle, and Mr. Gunn was wounded."

"Gunn has never talked about any of this before."

"I've always been told that true men prefer to forget about the time they spent at war and only those who didn't live up to their duty go around bragging about it. Mr. Gunn never spoke a thing about it whenever he visited the family." She tilted her head to the side. "You know, I think he may have served in your American Civil War as well."

"He did?"

"I think I remember mother saying something about it. But at that age, I was more interested in balls and suitors than a foreign war."

Regret swirled up in Elspeth's memory and she pressed her lips together, turning back to the stove. Athos had nothing to add, so for several long, painful minutes, the house was silent again. The silence sat heavily, making Elspeth more and more nervous.

She nearly sighed aloud in relief when Athos said, "So I've managed to marry a real British lady, have I?"

"Technically, yes," she answered, eager to get the conversation going again, as awkward as it was. She moved to the breadbox to see if they had anything to serve with the stew. A thought struck her, and she straightened. "Although, perhaps technically I'm not a lady anymore." Embarrassment at the thought heated her cheeks. She bent to check the breadbox, finding half a loaf of bread and two wooden horses.

"Why *technically* not?" Athos sprang up from his chair with more energy than was necessary. He moved to the table, finding a knife, and took the bread from her to slice it.

Elspeth handed over the bread, respecting Athos's right to have something to keep his hands busy too. She set about washing and drying a few plates and bowls so they could have something clean to eat out of.

"I was formally disowned," she said in a quiet voice, glancing down at the pump as she pumped water into the sink.

"Disowned?" Athos let his arms drop in the middle of slicing bread. "By your own family?"

Elspeth nodded sadly. "I suppose there's no point in keeping the truth from you," she said, half to herself, then turned to glance shyly at him. "I met an American, a man named Craig Valko, at a ball when I was just nineteen. We struck up a flirtation that lasted through the rest of the season, growing more...intense as the days rolled by. I believed I was in love and allowed him...liberties." She blushed fiercely. "He promised to take me away with him to America, so one night I packed a bag, snuck out, and sailed away with him."

"That must have taken a lot of courage." He seemed more impressed than shocked by her confession.

"Yes, well, I'm not sure that a foolish heart and the allurement of…pleasures can be acquainted with courage." She set two bowls on the counter and checked to see if the stew was ready.

"So did you marry him?" Athos asked, crossing around her to find butter for their bread.

"No." Elspeth lowered her head further. "As it turned out, when we reached New York City, he was greeted at the dock by his wife and three children."

Athos stumbled a step on his way back from the pantry. "He was *married*?"

"Very much so. A fact he failed to tell me."

"What an ass." He shook his head, carrying the butter to the kitchen table. He cleared off two places, then returned to the counter for the bread he'd sliced. "So why did he bring you all the way to America then?"

For some reason, she'd imagined it would be bitterly hard and shameful to tell this seven-year-old story to Athos, but he listened as though she was telling him a fairy tale. "He planned to set me up as his mistress. Mind you, he told his wife that he had brought me back from England as a governess for their children."

"So what did you do?" He carried the plates and cutlery to the table as she ladled stew into their bowls.

"I didn't know what to do," she confessed. "I didn't know anyone in America and I had no money to speak of. I was too shocked by the truth to contradict him. So I went home with them and pretended to be a governess."

"Shameless," Athos muttered, carrying the bowls to the table once Elspeth had filled them. "Not you, I mean," he quickly added. "That man, if a man he can be called. He's utterly without shame."

Elspeth joined him at the kitchen table. "Yes, well, I think that for a time there I was the one without shame. I let the charade continue when I should have stepped right back on the boat and gone home. Instead, I lived under that man's roof for eight months as an adulteress."

Athos—who had begun eating—paused with his spoon halfway to his mouth. "Did he make you…"

"Yes," she answered without looking him in the eye. "Until his wife caught us. Not that I took any joy in it by that point." She stirred her stew, her appetite gone. "I didn't feel I had any choice. I…I was trapped and frightened."

Athos was perfectly still for a few more seconds, then resumed eating. "Well, I'm glad you're here with me now and not still stuck in a terrible situation like that."

Elspeth snapped her eyes up to stare at him. He wasn't judging her. He wasn't condemning her. He was *glad* that she was there with him. Her mind reeled. She blinked rapidly, then finished her story. "Afterwards, I took cheap lodgings and wrote to my family, asking to come home. I received a reply that I was a disgrace and a blight on the family name, that the scandal had hurt my sisters' marriage prospects. Also that our friends and relations had been told I was struck by a carriage and killed."

"What?"

"I was also informed that my name had been struck from the family Bible."

"Oh, Elspeth, that's terrible." He reached across the table to squeeze her hand.

A lump formed in Elspeth's throat, but she swallowed it along with a mouthful of stew. "I was paid wages while working for…that man's family, and with eight months' experience, I applied for another position as a governess. I almost ran out of money before I could find such a position. New Yorkers had heard of me, and none of the respectable families would hire me. I've spent six and a half of the last seven years shifting from one socially-striving family to another. I'm afraid far too many of the men of those families were aware of what had happened in New York and assumed I was up for more than just tutoring their children and teaching them French."

"It never ceases to amaze me how dishonest and lecherous some men can be," Athos said, shaking his head. "I'd like to give them all a piece of my mind."

Again, Elspeth was stunned by Athos's capacity for forgiveness of her sins, or perhaps it was his ability to see the truth of what she'd been through and not just a soiled reputation. Whatever it was, sharing her troubles seemed to have softened the blow he'd had in losing the children.

"I'm certain Solomon will be able to help us," Athos said later as they two of them cleaned up from their meager feast. "Just wait until you meet him. Solomon isn't like anyone I've ever met before. He pulled himself up out of slavery—actual, real slavery—and is now one of the richest and most well-respected men in Haskell. If anyone can help us, he can."

Elspeth couldn't help but smile at his assessment. "You are a man of incredible faith, Athos Strong," she told him as they washed their dishes and put the food away.

"What, me?" He seemed truly stunned by her assessment.

"Yes, you. And you're incredibly understanding of people."

He shrugged. "I see all sorts of people getting off and

on the train every day, and I have for more than a decade. You learn a lot of things about a lot of people just by giving them a hand now and then."

"I pray that this time it's your turn to be given a hand."

He grinned and lowered his head just a bit in modesty at her comment. "Honestly, at the moment, aside from Solomon—and maybe Gunn—there's only one hand I need right now."

"Which one is that?"

He held out a hand to her. Heart fluttering, Elspeth took it. A shimmering tingle raced up her arm and straight into her heart. It only intensified at the confident smile he gave her.

It was still fairly early, so for a short while, they made an attempt to tidy up the house. That included cleaning up the dining room at last. The night was dark and the house eerily quiet by the time they climbed the stairs for bed. Neither of them said much as they changed out of their worn clothes and into nightclothes. In the back of Elspeth's mind, she wondered if now was the right time to suggest they consummate their marriage. After the wretched day they'd just had, it might bring them both a measure of comfort.

"Sleep well tonight, Mrs. Strong," Athos said without a hint of flirtation as he climbed into bed. "We're going to need all of our energy tomorrow so we can get those kids back."

The growing tension inside of Elspeth floated away with a fond smile. "You're right." She climbed into bed beside him and blew out the lantern on her side of the bed.

Darkness and quiet enveloped them. It was like the calm before the storm, the eye of the hurricane. It was sad and gloomy without bumps and whispers and shuffling from children in the house. The noises outside seemed too close and her thoughts were too loud. All Elspeth had to anchor herself to was Athos's breathing.

Athos. Kind, powerful, tragic Athos.

She rolled over, facing him as he lay on his back, eyes closed, breathing steady. A tremor passed through her heart as she scooted closer to him and rested an arm over his chest. He sucked in a breath, then let it out on a tranquil hum, then hugged her close. Elspeth closed her eyes and willed herself to fall asleep. She would need all the rest she could get now. Tomorrow the battle would begin.

Athos was certain he wouldn't sleep a wink that night, not when the house was so quiet, not when his heart was at the hotel. But a strange thing happened when Elspeth inched closer and tucked her arm around him. His muscles loosened, his worries lightened, and sleep overtook him. The last, fleeting thought that passed through his mind was that it was nice to have a pretty woman who believed in him cuddled in his arms.

The next morning, he awoke with a smile on his face, almost convinced that everything was all right. Elspeth still slumbered against his side. He shifted to slid an arm around her, wondering if he might be able to get away with greeting the morning by doing what married people usually did in bed. If he was quiet, the kids wouldn't even—

The reality that he found himself in swung back on him with a thump. The children. They'd been taken. They were at the hotel. He had to get them back.

He sat up with a start, waking Elspeth in the process.

"What? What is it?" she asked, bleary with sleep, pushing herself to sit up by his side. The neck of her nightgown sagged delicately, giving him the briefest glimpse of her breasts, but even that wasn't enough to calm the surge of panic that launched him out of bed.

"We have to go back to the hotel to see the children," he said, racing for the washstand.

"Of course." Elspeth rushed to get out of bed as well, then turned to carefully make it.

Any other day, Athos would have said something about how tidy she was and how kind to make the bed first thing, but all he could focus on right then was getting dressed. He didn't even bother shaving.

"We need to speak to Solomon, like Gunn suggested," he spoke half to himself as he pulled on the first clean trousers he put his hands on.

"Solomon Templesmith." Elspeth repeated the name as if quizzing herself on all the new people she'd met. Her clothes were still folded in her traveling trunk against the wall. She pulled out a dress and shook it, then sighed as the wrinkles didn't come out. "It'll just have to do," she murmured to herself.

A grin quirked at the corner of Athos's mouth. "I bet a real lady like you had an army of servants to take care of things like your clothes when you were growing up."

Elspeth sent him one wary look and said, "We did."

Athos's brow flew up, and he turned his back to give Elspeth a shred of privacy. "Servants! Imagine that."

He couldn't think of anything else to say as he searched for a clean shirt and put it on. What did you say to a real lady anyhow? What did you say to a wife, for that matter? He never really had mastered the art of *talking* to Natalie. Those first few years they were too young and done in by circumstance to figure out what to say to each other. After that, there were too many mouths to feed and clothes to wash and shoes to tie. And it was just his luck that the only way he'd ever discovered of communing with Natalie usually ended up with more children.

"I'll wait for you downstairs," he said, cheeks red, once he finished dressing. Heaven only knew how many children they'd end up having if he and Elspeth started *communing*. "We can head over to the hotel directly."

Elspeth finished pulling her dress over her head as he reached the door and caught him with, "Aren't we going to have breakfast?"

He paused, considering, then nodded. "I'll toast some bread and make some tea. There's no time to lose."

Toast and tea would have to be enough to start things off. Every second that Athos spent away from his children was torture. To her credit, Elspeth was quick to finish dressing and fixing her hair—which hung in one simple braid down her back—and to join him downstairs. Neither of them said anything as they downed their quick breakfast, then headed out.

"I have to make one stop first," he told her, turning right once he got to the street instead of left, which would have led them up to the hotel. He took her hand and set out at a fast walk. "It's Saturday, so there's only one train coming through today, but someone has to be there to unload it."

They marched all the way down Prairie Avenue to Station Street, then around the corner and a few feet up Main Street until they came to Haskell's jail. Athos could see that Elspeth was baffled by the stop, but he didn't have time to explain. He rapped on the door, then pushed it open.

"Trey?" He called into the empty room. There wasn't even a drunk locked up in the cell. It must have been a quiet night.

A thump and then footsteps sounded from the

second floor. A few seconds later, Sheriff Trey Knighton stomped down the staircase on one side of the room…in his long johns. He squinted with sleep and hadn't shaved. That, combined with the fierce look he wore at being woken up, caused Elspeth to flinch. She had a point. With the vicious scar that cut across Trey's face, he looked more like he should be in the cell than wearing the star.

But there wasn't time for introductions or explanations either.

"Trey, I need you to do me a favor." Athos launched right into his mission.

"Huh?" Trey grunted, rubbing his face. "Athos, do you know what time it is?"

Athos ignored the question. "I need you to keep an eye on the station today and unload the train if it comes in before I get back."

"Okay." Trey sounded dubious. "I don't really know what to do, other than being extra muscle when you need it." He blinked, eyes widening as he noticed Elspeth standing with hands clasped in front of her by Athos's side.

"It's easy. The train's porter should know what needs to be unloaded in Haskell. All you need to do is move it to the warehouse and not let anyone take anything before I can get back to inventory it."

"Sure, but—"

"Sorry, we have to go." One tiny speck of worry lifted from his shoulders. He turned and took Elspeth's hand again, starting out of the jail.

"Hey, hold on, Athos. What's going on?" Trey stepped after them.

"Bonneville had some government lady take my kids away," Athos replied, voice grim and edged with anger. "They're at the hotel, and I'm going to get them back."

Trey muttered a curse as Athos and Elspeth rushed back out into Main Street. Athos should have gone back and made him apologize to Elspeth for using language in front of her, but Trey's gritty streak was the least of his concerns right then.

They charged up Main Street, Athos's temper growing hotter with each step. It was a stroke of luck that as they passed in front of the bank, Solomon threw open his door and strode out to join them as if he had been keeping a look out in case they stopped by.

"Gunn told me what's going on," he said without preamble. "He showed me the court order too."

"He did?" Athos slowed his steps to walk at Solomon's stately pace. He hadn't been aware that he'd left the parchment with Gunn the day before. He hadn't been aware of a lot of things. Like Elspeth panting at his side. "Oh! I'm sorry. Solomon, I'd like you to meet my new wife, Elspeth. Elspeth, this is Solomon Templesmith."

"Pleased to meet you." Miraculously, Elspeth managed to complete a ladylike curtsy for Solomon as they walked on.

Solomon greeted her curtsy with a noble nod and a tip of his hat. "Ma'am. I'm only sorry that we had to meet under such trying circumstances."

The fleeting thought that Elspeth and Solomon might just be the two most dignified people Athos knew passed through is mind before it latched on to other things. "Do you think Bonneville and that woman could really take my children from me?"

"No," Solomon answered, but he wasn't as confident as Athos wanted him to be. "At least, I don't think the appeals judge—or any other judge who actually met you and the children and saw the way things are with you— would uphold this bogus order."

"Good," Elspeth exclaimed. When Solomon glanced at her, she went on. "It's the most ridiculous thing I've ever seen. I've been a governess in one household after another for the past several years, and I can assure you that the Strong children are happier and healthier than a good deal of other children."

Solomon grinned and nodded. "I may call on you to give that testimony at the hearing."

They reached the hotel and entered together, as a unified group ready to fight for what was right. Athos let go of Elspeth's hand and surged forward the second he caught a glimpse of the back of Heather's head in the hotel's dining room. He marched straight on, heedless of the hotel staff members who jumped into high alert or the patrons who raised curious eyebrows to see what was happening.

"I've come to take my children back," Athos announced as soon as he burst into the dining room.

What had been a normal breakfast for hotel patrons and townspeople alike screeched to a halt. All eight of the Strong children sat at a long table at the far end of the room. Mrs. Lyon presided at the head of the table. She had a full plate of eggs, sausage, ham, and fruit in front of her, while each of the children had nothing but bowls of plain oatmeal. The four thugs stood at the four corners of the table. The rest of the restaurant contained a handful of tables of diners...including the Bonnevilles. Bonnie Horner sat by Rex Bonneville's side. She rose from her place with a triumphant smile as soon as Athos made his declaration.

"Papa! Papa!" The table with the Strong children burst into chaos. The older ones were able to leap out of their seats and run to him while the younger ones squirmed and struggled to get down.

"Sweethearts." Athos managed to catch Ivy and Heather in a tight hug, kissing the tops of their heads, before the thugs separated them. The younger children hadn't even made it away from the table before they were nabbed and forced back into their places.

"What is the meaning of this?" Mrs. Lyon snarled, throwing down her napkin and standing.

"I could ask the same thing," Athos said. "How dare you rip my children away from me?"

The kids all continued to shout.

"Papa!"

"Take us home, Papa!"

"I don't like it here."

"I want to go home."

Athos started toward Vernon—who stood closest now that Ivy and Heather had been wrestled back to the table—but Bonneville jumped up from his seat to stop him.

"Obstruction of justice as well as dereliction of parental duty? Eh, Strong?" Bonneville seethed with a sly smile.

"This is your fault, Bonneville." Athos balled a fist and pivoted to face the man.

The Bonneville daughters yelped in fear, and Solomon barked a quick, "Don't." It was Elspeth's light touch on Athos's arm that drained his need to punch Bonneville.

"Ooh, he's horrible," Bebe squealed, bursting into tears.

"How could a noble *lady* debase herself by marrying him?" Melinda added.

"He's always been very kind and responsible," Honoria mentioned.

"Shut up, Honoria," Vivian snapped.

"Girls," Bonnie warned them, but aside from Honoria, the Bonneville sisters merely turned up their noses at her and got up to watch the scene unfolding.

"I want to go home," Geneva whined, starting a new wave of protest from the children. They seemed to thrive on the complaints, encouraging each other to be as loud and irritating as they could be.

"I want something better than oatmeal to eat," Thomas hollered above the rest of them. "She gets sausage, so how come we only get yucky oatmeal? It doesn't even have brown sugar."

Athos whipped back to Mrs. Lyon. "Are you attempting to starve my children?"

Mrs. Lyon sniffed and tilted her chin up. "Children should be fed a simple diet that will not aggravate their already irascible spirits."

"But I like sausage," Lael complained.

"You want sausage? I'll get you sausage," Hubert declared. He darted behind Mr. Lyon before any of the thugs could stop them and grabbed not only the sausages, but a handful of eggs straight from her plate. "Here."

He tossed the entire handful to Lael, who caught the sausage with a sudden laugh. The eggs splattered on the floor.

"How *dare* you?" Mrs. Lyon blanched.

"Like this," Ivy said. She broke out of the grip of the surprised thug who held her arm and scooped her hand into the nearest oatmeal bowl. With a satisfied grunt, she threw the handful at the thug's face. "We will not be cowed!" she declared, just as the hero in the book they'd been reading had.

That was all it took to thrust the scene into pandemonium. All of the Strong children that were not being physically restrained lunged for their oatmeal bowls. In a matter of seconds, large globs of lukewarm oatmeal were flying all through the restaurant. The Bonneville sisters screamed and tried to flee the dining room, but their movement only made them targets. Vivian elbowed Honoria in her attempt to bolt, sending her crashing against Solomon. Solomon grabbed her and held her up, but in his effort to counterbalance, he thrust out a foot, which tripped Melinda.

The thugs rushed to try to restrain as many of the children as possible, but they were outnumbered. Hubert and Millie managed to wriggle away and set about grabbing and throwing whatever food they could get their hands on from any of the tables in the restaurant. A stray piece of bacon hit Athos in the head, followed by Millie's overexcited, "Sorry, Papa."

It wasn't until Athos spotted Gunn sprinting for the restaurant that he shouted, "Children, stop!"

Instantly, all eight of the kids froze where they were. Their eyes glittered brightly, as if they would burst into action again as soon as he gave the word.

"This is an outrage!" Mrs. Lyon shouted.

"It certainly is," Bonneville agreed. His daughters hadn't made it out of the room, and now three of them stood huddled together weeping in frustration, as Honoria continued to hide her face against Solomon's shoulder. "I demand action be taken at once."

"So do I," Athos joined the fray. "I demand that my children be returned home this instant."

"They should all be locked up in jail," Vivian whined.

"Or a pigpen," Melinda added.

"No one is being locked in any jails." Gunn intervened the moment he reached the restaurant. "I'll take the children back up to their rooms and—"

"No!" Mrs. Lyon thundered.

Gunn turned to her, brow raised in horror, eyes flashing with indignation.

"This was a mistake," Mrs. Lyon went on, not recognizing the danger she'd stepped into.

"It *was* a mistake," Athos panted. "Return my children to me at once."

"It was a mistake to lodge the children at this hotel, so close to the disruptive influence of their father."

"What?" Elspeth stepped forward. "That's absurd. He's their father. He has a right to see his children."

"Not if it incites them to behavior such as this," Mrs. Lyon growled.

In the back of Athos's mind, it dawned on him that letting his children run riot, even if it was in defense of him, wasn't necessarily the right way to convince the world they should be returned to him.

"The children should be lodged somewhere far from that man's influence," Mrs. Lyon went on, thrusting a finger at Athos. "They should not have any contact with him at all."

"That's not fair," Heather called out.

"He's our father," Ivy added.

"Let us go," Hubert rounded out the complaint.

"No." Mrs. Lyon stomped to underline her point. A diabolical light flashed in her eyes. "No, you all are behaving like perfect animals, so you should be kept where those animals are kept."

"Yes, a pigpen," Melinda exclaimed.

"Lock them in a stable," Bebe added.

"I still think they should be in jail," Vivian muttered.

"Are you going to put us in a zoo?" Thomas asked, his question somewhat hopeful.

Mrs. Lyon ignored him, crossing in front of Athos and Elspeth, stepping over splotches of oatmeal and scrambled eggs on the carpet, until she reached the Bonneville cluster. "No, the children should be secured on a ranch until such a time as my order can be enforced. You own a ranch, I believe, Mr. Bonneville."

Stunned silence fell over the Bonneville sisters.

"You can't mean that they should live at our house until the judge takes them away?" Vivian squeaked.

"That is exactly what I mean." Mrs. Lyon nodded. "As I understand it, your ranch is a sufficient distance from town, you have many ranch hands who could prevent Mr. Strong from interfering, and," she rounded on Rex Bonneville, "you were the one who lodged the complaint."

Athos's temper flared. He clenched his fists and inched forward to protest.

Out of the corner of his eye, he caught sight of Gunn…grinning. It gave him pause. Frustrated and confused, he sent a questioning look Gunn's way.

Still grinning as if Mrs. Lyon had just told a riotous joke, he met Athos's eyes and shook his head.

Athos let out a breath, as confused as ever. Then again, if Gunn thought it was a good idea—a *funny* idea— that his children should be taken out to the Bonneville ranch, then maybe it was. He could just imagine Bonneville and his spoiled daughters trying to put up with Vernon and Lael's antics or Thomas's constant questions or Ivy and Heather's emotional turns. He blinked, grinning himself. Why, if the Bonnevilles had to deal with his kids for more than a few days, they'd be sending them back in no time.

"I agree," he said, nodding and crossing his arms.

"What?" Vivian snapped, looking downright sick.

"I agree that the children would be safest at the Bonneville ranch," Athos repeated.

The children turned to him, stunned.

"But…but Papa."

"I want to go home."

"The Bonneville ranch?"

"If you can't stay at home with me until the judge gets here—" Athos started.

"On Friday," Gunn interrupted. Everyone assembled turned to him in surprise. "I've just had a telegram," Gunn went on. "Judge Andrew Moss will be here on Friday."

"That's less than a week," Elspeth said, eyes bright.

Athos reached for her hand, squeezing it. "I agree that the children should stay at the Bonneville ranch until Friday."

"That's not what was supposed to happen," Bebe blurted.

"You can't make us take these vagrants in," Melinda sniffed.

"I wouldn't mind taking care of them for a few days." Honoria stepped away from Solomon and smiled tentatively at the kids.

"Shut up, Honoria," Vivian sighed.

"You were the one who instigated these proceedings," Mrs. Lyon reminded Rex.

A moment of expectant silence followed as they all turned to Rex Bonneville.

Rex clenched his jaw, narrowed his eyes, and held his breath. He glared at Athos and at Solomon. Then he said in a tight voice, "All right. They can come to my ranch. But if they break or destroy anything, you're paying for it," he spat at Athos, then turned to march out of the room.

"Yeah, you'll pay for it," Bebe repeated, then tilted her nose in the air and followed her father out.

Melinda and Vivian did the same. Honoria glanced after them, then skipped over to Athos.

"I'll watch out for them." Her promise was followed by a racking cough.

"Miss Honoria, perhaps you should see Dr. Meyers about that cough before you head home," Solomon suggested.

"It's nothing." Honoria smiled up at him, cheeks pink, then fled the room.

"Gentlemen, prepare the children to be taken to the Bonneville ranch," Mrs. Lyon ordered her thugs.

"Yes, ma'am," they answered, then began to herd the kids out of the restaurant.

The kids didn't go without protest, though.

"I'm scared," Geneva confessed.

"Me too," Millicent echoed.

"I'll make them regret ever taking us," Hubert vowed.

"No." Athos held out his hand and shook his head. "Children, you have to behave while you're at the Bonneville ranch."

"What?" Vernon and Lael protested.

"That's no fun." Ivy exchanged a wicked glance with her twin.

"Trust me." Athos shuffled into the lobby, Elspeth following, as the thugs pushed the children on. "I think Mr. Gunn and Mr. Templesmith, Elspeth and I are about to hatch a plan to bring you home."

"Yay!" The younger children shouted.

"Quiet!" Mrs. Lyon snapped. She made sure the children were pushed to the back hall where they'd had their scene the day before.

It was near torture for Athos to let them go. Heart aching, he turned back to Gunn and Solomon. He reached for Elspeth's hand, and once he held it tight, he asked, "What do we do?"

Chapter Seven

Throughout the entire, chaotic scene in the restaurant, Elspeth stood by Athos's side. It didn't take a genius to see that there was so much more to the conflict in front of them than children's behavior or the kind of father Athos was. The Bonneville family was a stunning example of how clean dresses and perfect posture meant nothing if what was inside the package was rotten. The only Bonneville that Elspeth didn't find completely repugnant was Honoria, but even an outsider could see that the shy young woman didn't stand a chance against her ill-mannered, vindictive sisters.

"The Bonnevilles are crafty," Solomon said in answer to Athos's question. He gestured for Athos and her to follow him to a quieter corner of the lobby as Mr. Gunn fretfully gathered his staff to clean up the mess that had been made of his restaurant. "So we have to be craftier."

"How?" The tell-tale signs that the entire catastrophe was taking its toll could be seen in the tension bunching Athos's shoulders and the desperation lining his face.

Solomon extended a hand to a small sofa in the

lobby's corner, inviting Elspeth and Athos to sit. He took a seat kitty-corner to them in a chair. "We're already off to a good start. I don't think the Bonnevilles expected to be saddled with the children."

"They certainly didn't," Elspeth said, bringing to mind the shock and horror on the sisters' faces.

Athos reached for her hand and squeezed it. He'd been holding her hand a lot in the last day, just like Thomas had when his siblings were all at school and he hadn't quite known what to do with himself.

"They'll get a taste of what it's like to parent eight children, that's for sure," Solomon went on. "But we must also find a way to get word to them that they must behave like perfect angels while they're out there on the ranch."

"What?" Elspeth and Athos asked at the same time. They exchanged a look of surprised that they'd answered in chorus, then gave their attention back to Solomon.

"Hear me out." Solomon raised his hands. "The complaint that was taken to the court in Cheyenne alleges that the children are out-of-control as well as being neglected and mismanaged."

"They're not," Athos insisted. "They're just lively, interested children."

"I know that," Solomon went on, "but if the appeals judge had witnessed the scene we just saw, what conclusions do you think he would draw?"

Elspeth's shoulder sagged with delayed embarrassment over the food fight. "I can see why having them behave in front of the judge would be helpful," she said, "but how does good behavior while at the Bonneville ranch benefit us?" She would have thought that the case to return the children to Athos as quickly as possible would have been better made if they drove the Bonneville sisters to the brink of insanity.

One peep at Athos told her he thought the same thing. "I doubt they're displaying church manners right now."

"Then you need to figure out a way to go out to the ranch and tell them," Solomon said. "If the children are clever enough to change the Bonneville sisters' minds, make them think that they're the sweetest bunch of angels that ever graced the earth, then they might retract their complaint before the judge even gets here."

"But what about that Lyon woman?" Athos asked. "She seems like a real shrew, and not particularly likely to give up now that she's got the bit between her teeth."

"Ah, but she's not the one who brought the case before the courts," Solomon explained. "She was merely sent to fulfill the judge's order. Once the appeals judge makes a ruling, she will have to abide by it."

"Then you're right." Elspeth sat straighter. "All we need to do is convince this appeals judge that the case is frivolous and was brought about out of revenge for imagined wrongs, and he'll side with Athos and the children will be returned."

"Exactly." Solomon smiled, studying Elspeth. "I heard a rumor that Charlie, Virginia, and Josephine had picked out a remarkable bride for Athos, but I see now that the rumors didn't come close to the truth."

Elspeth blushed and looked down. "I've hardly been here long enough to be the subject of rumors."

Solomon smirked. "This is Haskell." That seemed to be explanation enough. "At this rate, I should get them to send for a bride for me."

"You're thinking of marrying?" Athos asked.

Solomon shrugged. "The nights can get quiet."

"Tell me about it." Athos heaved a sigh. "So other than making sure the children know to behave while they're with Bonneville, what else can we do?"

"Whatever it takes to make the judge see that you're an excellent father."

"Make the judge *believe* I'm an excellent father, you mean."

Solomon gave Athos a curious look. "That's what I said. Tidy up your house, plant a few flowers in the garden, and make sure everyone is ready to present a good case once Judge Moss arrives on Friday."

"Tidy the house," Elspeth repeated. The piles of laundry, stacks of dirty dishes, and mountains of toys loomed in her mind. And she hadn't really had time to investigate the children's rooms.

"That's it." Solomon slapped his knees and stood. Athos and Elspeth stood with him. "You two take care of your end, and I'll build an eloquent case from my end."

"Thank you, Solomon." Athos reached out to shake his hand. "I don't know what I would do without you."

Solomon shook hands, then thumped Athos on the back. "There are a lot of people in this town who will rush to help you, Athos. You'll see." He let go of Athos's hand and turned to Elspeth. "Mrs. Strong." With a nod, he started off, striding through the lobby with so much confidence that he bolstered Elspeth's spirits.

"I hope he's right," Athos murmured.

Elspeth turned to him, heart aching. "I'm sure he is. Now, let's go home and get started on the tidying. I think it might take until Friday to get the house looking its best."

She intended her words to be a joke, but a middle-aged woman passing through the lobby who had overheard snorted. Elspeth frowned at the woman.

Seeing she'd been caught eavesdropping, the woman threw up her hands. "The day Athos Strong keeps a handle on his children is the day pigs fly."

Elspeth's jaw dropped. "Excuse me, ma'am, but I don't believe you have an informed opinion on the matter."

The woman stopped in her tracks and planted her hands on her hips. "An informed opinion? I live across the way from that lot of heathens. I hear the kind of racket they make and see the mess they leave everywhere they go."

"It's not as bad as all that, Mrs. Plover," Athos assured her.

"It is so," Mrs. Plover replied. "And frankly, it's about time someone stepped in. Those Bonnevilles have the right idea, if you ask me." She ended with a humph, then marched on to the restaurant.

Stunned, Elspeth moved with Athos as he shook his head and walked away, out of the hotel and into the street. They were halfway home before he said, "Mrs. Plover is probably right."

"She is not," Elspeth snapped.

Athos popped his head up from where it was bowed in thought. A tired smile spread across his face. "Thanks for saying that. It means a lot." He didn't say it, but Elspeth felt "but she's still right," was just behind those words.

They continued on without saying much more. The house wasn't in any better order now than it had been when they left. Elspeth tried to look at it with new eyes, with the eyes of Judge Moss. It did look a little cluttered and overwhelmed.

"All we have to do is put all of the toys and clothes and things away, then scrub it from top to bottom," she speculated as they walked up onto the porch. "I can do that while you're at work."

"Work," Athos sighed as though just remembering it.

"I have to work while all of this is going on." He shoved a hand through his hair then rubbed his face. "And now I have to try to get through everything at work without Hubert. I doubt that Lyon woman will let him help after school like he has been doing."

"Well, we'll worry about that problem when we come to it." Elspeth took a deep breath, willing herself to be confident. They knew what they had to do, after all. She headed down the hall. "Let's start cleaning with the kitchen."

"I should really go back to the train station," Athos said, following her anyhow.

"What time is today's train scheduled to arrive?"

"Eleven forty-five."

She smiled over her shoulder at him. "Then you have a little bit of time to help me get started. Sheriff Knighton is keeping an eye out, after all, and I believe you could use a bit of time to sort out your thoughts."

They crossed into the kitchen. Some of Elspeth's certainty wavered as she glanced around at the jumble of dirty dishes interspersed with toys and books that waited for them.

"You're right." Athos sighed, then chuckled. "What is it about women that makes them always right about things?"

Elspeth laughed. "Maybe it's our feminine wiles." She made up her mind to start washing dishes first and headed to the sink.

Athos started his work by clearing the kitchen table and sorting the toys from the books from a few inexplicable items of clothing that had found their way into the mess. "Or maybe it's something that wives pick up as soon as they say their vows," he went on. "Natalie always used to be able to tell when something was bothering me, even if we hadn't had time to speak to each other in days."

Elspeth's hand fumbled on the pump. "You didn't speak to your wife for days?" She hid the itchy feeling that she'd trod on someone's grave by working the pump to fill the sink.

"Not on purpose," Athos went on, moving around the kitchen to put things away. "I was so busy and she was so busy that sometimes our paths didn't cross for a day or two."

"That's...that's awful."

"I suppose so." Athos paused, and Elspeth caught him frowning, eyes unfocused. "I'm not sure Natalie would have married me if she had the choice."

Elspeth's brow flew up. "Why ever not?"

He shrugged and went back to work. "She was in love with someone else back home, a friend of mine, Robert. Robert took a fancy to another girl, though, and it broke Natalie's heart. I felt bad about the whole thing because I saw it coming, so I did what any friend would do and gave her a shoulder to cry on. Only, somehow that turned into a little more than a shoulder."

Another pause followed. Elspeth glanced up from the soapy water in the sink to find that Athos's face had gone bright red. He caught her staring at him in question and went on with, "We were married and Hubert came along six months after the wedding."

It was Elspeth's turn to blush. "I see." She plunged her hands into the sink again, scrubbing away. It wasn't right for her to be shocked that Athos would get a girl in trouble, not with her past being what it was, but it was unexpected. What wasn't unexpected was that he'd done the right thing and married her.

"I was nineteen at the time," Athos went on, stacking a few clean dishes that had ended up on the table on the shelf to one side of the room. "Natalie was a few weeks shy of her eighteenth birthday."

"You were so young," Elspeth exclaimed.

Athos chuckled. "I'm only thirty-five now. How else would someone my age have eight children, the oldest of which is sixteen?"

"Good point."

"And anyhow, I think Natalie was happy with the way things turned out." He finished stacking the dishes, then filled his arms with toys. "I was already working for the railroad by that point, and as soon as I was offered a job out West, she encouraged me to take it. I think she wanted to get away from Hartford."

"Why? That was your home."

"A home where she would have had to live every day with her neighbors knowing that she'd…slipped," he pointed out. "And where Robert and his wife would always be living down the street. I actually think she wanted to get away from that more than the shame of what we'd done. I think she still…"

He shook his head, then left the room with his arms full of toys. Elspeth listened to his footfalls as he carried them upstairs, presumably to put them in the proper child's bedroom. A seed of anger had sprouted in her gut, and she scrubbed a few pots with extra vigor. She'd never met Natalie and couldn't now, but she wondered if she would have liked the woman. By Athos's account, she hadn't appreciated what she'd had. Elspeth was certain Athos was worth a hundred Roberts, a hundred anyones. At least she had appreciated him enough to give him eight wonderful children.

Children who were being carted out to the Bonneville

ranch—wherever that was—right that minute. Children who were potentially frightened and definitely angry. Children who she had let down before she had had the chance to really get to know them.

She sighed, stepping to the side for a moment to dry and put away the dishes she'd washed, making room for the rest that were still dirty. It wasn't right to fault Natalie for her imagined shortcomings when she hadn't been able to protect the woman's children. Natalie must have done something right, because underneath their energy and mischievousness, the Strong children truly were exceptional.

"You don't want to see what the bedrooms look like," Athos said as he walked back into the room, startling Elspeth out of her thoughts. "I should have made them clean up a little more often."

"Is it that bad?" If she focused on concrete things instead of regrets, maybe her heart wouldn't break.

Athos smirked. "We might need shovels. At least we won't have to worry about Piper's attic."

They continued to work. Athos cleared away the last remaining mess in the dining room, bringing her a few dishes that had escaped notice the day before. As hard as she scrubbed or as focused as she tried to be on cleaning, Elspeth couldn't shake the sensation that the house was too quiet. Maybe it wasn't just the missing children. Maybe Natalie's ghost was scolding her for letting Mrs. Lyon sweep in and destroy everything.

"How did you end up with such an interesting name?" she asked when she couldn't stand the oppressive quiet anymore.

"Athos?" Athos straightened from where he was rearranging the shelves in the pantry, on the other side of an open doorway, to make room for the boxes and cans that had been living on kitchen counters. "It's from Alexander Dumas' *The Three Musketeers*. My father was an avid reader, and Dumas' stories were some of his favorite. *The Three Musketeers* was being published in serial form around the time I was born."

"I see. So you're literary then?"

He laughed. "I don't have time to read, other than the dime novels I get to read to the kids at night." His words trailed off to sadness for a moment. He cleared his throat, then continued. "My father used to read to us every night too. I think he read *The Three Musketeers* five times before I was ten. I always used to dream that I would be a musketeer."

"Did you?"

"Yeah." He huffed a soft laugh. His hands stilled on the shelves, and he stared off at nothing. "I always thought I would be a daring hero, running around the country protecting the king. Of course, that was before I realized America had a president." He laughed and returned to work organizing the shelves. "I used to carry a wooden sword around with me wherever I went."

Elspeth burst into a smile. "I can imagine that."

He chuckled. "All I wanted to do was fight for what was right and good, defend the land, and have adventures. What I ended up doing was going to work right out of school, marrying too young and starting a family, and dedicating my life to the railroad."

She put the last of the scrubbed plates on the counter to dry. "I'd say that's pretty adventurous."

"Really?"

She turned to lean her hip against the counter, crossing her arms. "Yes. Absolutely. You left everything to come out West and begin a new life."

"Because that's where my job sent me," he qualified.

"I wasn't a brave pioneer, like Howard Haskell and his family."

"I don't know." Elspeth shrugged. "It takes a lot of courage to say yes when your employer sends you out into the frontier."

He finished his work, then stepped into the doorway, leaning against the frame. "Maybe. But keeping your nose to the grindstone while your children get older and your wife grows distant isn't exactly the sort of thing Dumas wrote about."

Between his words and the wistful look in his eyes, it felt as though a vise had grabbed hold of Elspeth's heart. She noticed, possibly for the first time, that he had the clearest hazel eyes she'd ever seen. Plenty of other women would have found him too stocky and unkempt to be handsome, but there was something noble, something tender about him all the same.

She pushed away from the counter and crossed to close her arms around him in a hug. Athos drew in a breath in surprise, tensing for a second. Then he let that tension go and laughed.

"What's that all about?" he asked as she leaned back to study his face.

"You looked like you needed it," she answered.

He looked into her eyes, really looked. Something beyond sadness and defeat glowed there. Yes, she could see it. Behind those clear hazel eyes and scruffy face lurked Athos the Musketeer.

A moment later, he blinked, and an even deeper emotion flared to life. With a soft rush of breath, he dipped closer to her. His eyelids lowered as his lips sought out hers. She surged up to meet him with a thrill of gladness in her heart that she couldn't explain. He kissed her gently at first, then with an increasing rush of intensity. His lips parted hers with more boldness than she would have guessed he had, and his tongue sought out hers. His arms tightened around her, one hand brushing her side close to her breast.

In a moment, the world was spinning for joy as she pressed against him. Athos Strong was deceptive. His kiss was passionate, his arms firm with muscle, and his embrace full of promise. Excitement zipped through her as she felt him stiffen against her hip. The sudden, mad urge to reach for him and give him the pleasure her soul felt he'd been missing from his life was almost irresistible. They could be exceptionally good together. Her heart and the experiences of her past whispered that temptation in her ear. But unlike her shameful past mistakes, she and Athos were married.

The distant cry of a train whistle blasted through their moment of intimacy as swiftly as a cannon. Athos jumped back, panting and flushed.

"It's early," he gasped, at odds with the picture he presented.

"What?" Elspeth blinked rapidly, pressing a hand to her pounding heart.

"The eleven forty-five. It's early." He leapt into motion, rushing out of the pantry and heading for the hall and the front door. "I have to be there if I can," he went on, frantic and blabbering. "Trey is a good friend, but he really doesn't know how to meet a train. It's more than just unloading the cargo and passengers. There are things to be recorded, messages to send back to switching stations and central depots. I really should ask for an assistant. This sort of thing needs to get done, and I should be there."

When he reached the front door, he pivoted to give Elspeth one final look. The heat was still in his eyes.

"That was nice," he said, reaching for the door handle. "We…we should do that again sometime."

"Yes, we should," Elspeth answered.

But he was already rushing out the door, like a schoolboy, giddy over his first kiss.

Chapter Eight

She was standing by his side, her hair wreathed in summer daisies, the way it had been for their wedding. The sun shone merrily down on a green church lawn. The air was scented with honeysuckle and roses. Every part of him was warm from his head to his toes...and one important area in between. The minister murmured dreamlike words, and he knew the time had come for him to kiss his bride. He turned to her, drawing her into his arms and slanting his mouth over hers. She responded with open affection, looping her arms around his neck. His body sang with need as their tongues twined, as they pressed against each other. He was ready, aching with need, heart bursting.

Only when he leaned back to smile at his wife, it was Elspeth's beautiful face he saw, not Natalie's.

Athos awoke with a start. It wasn't the first time he had dreamed of that wedding day, far more idealized than it had actually been. Dreams about Natalie were common enough. They'd spent over a decade together, after all.

Dreams about Elspeth were something else entirely.

In his dream, she had been so, so beautiful. So alive and welcoming. Like she had been the day before when he'd kissed her. He'd carried that kiss with him through the entire rest of the day, tasting her lips on his, feeling the softness of her curves pressed against him. One kiss, and Elspeth had stirred something to life in him that had—

He sucked in a breath. He was hard as a rock. Hot, pulsing need had him at full attention. And heaven help him, it felt good. Waking with an erection was common enough, but not one this strong. The delicious fullness had him stretched and sensitive...and half out of his mind to know what to do about it. Thank God he lay on his side with his back to Elspeth. Even if she was awake—which he doubted based on the steadiness of her breathing—she wouldn't be able to see the mammoth tent he was likely to make of the blankets if he had been lying on his back.

Elspeth. He could smell her feminine scent, feel the heat of her body only inches away from his. The gentle rush of her breath against the pillow and the brush of her arm against his back told him she lay on her side facing him. He could twist to face her. He could keep going and roll her to her back. He could lift up her nightgown and graze his hands against the silky-smooth flesh of her inner thighs, parting her legs. She would probably be wet and ready, the furnace of her desire stoked even hotter than what he'd felt when they kissed the day before. He could slide between her thighs and glide—

He stifled a moan as his erection twitched. Another part of him wanted to laugh out loud. When was the last time he'd felt this kind of anticipation, this heady lust? Arousal was a dangerous game to play when young children might bounce into the room at any second and crawl into bed with you. That wasn't a problem at the moment.

A devilish thought struck him. Flushing hot with desire and daring, he slowly inched his hand down to the drawstring of his drawers. He paused to listen, checking to see if Elspeth had awaken yet. Everything was still, so he tugged on the string. It came loose. He paused to listen again. Still nothing. He swallowed and reached into his drawers.

A long, hungry sigh escaped from his lungs as he wrapped his hand around his swollen shaft and gave it a gentle tug. Too long. It had been too long since he'd done even that. It was a pale, pale imitation of what he really wanted. He wanted to bury himself deep inside of his wife, Elspeth's perfect, willing body. He wanted to kiss her and stroke her and show her all of the things he'd learned in a decade of trying to make up for not being the man Natalie wanted to marry. He wanted to make Elspeth sigh and whimper as he brought her pleasure like—

"What's the matter?"

Her piercing question came simultaneously with his release. His groan of completion ended up sounding more like a shout of terror. He thanked his lucky stars for the blankets covering him and twisted to look over his shoulder at her.

"Nothing?" he squeaked, panting.

One wide-eyed look from Elspeth and he knew he couldn't hide anything. It didn't help that a fine sweat had broken out on his brow and he was hot enough to guess he was bright red. The fact that he kept his hand well under the covers probably gave things away too.

Elspeth's shock hung on for another second before her lips twitched. She snorted, eyes dancing with mirth, then slapped a hand to her mouth.

Athos squeezed his eyes shut, praying that in spite of

her experience she didn't know enough about men to guess how they played with themselves.

His prayer fell on deaf ears as she scooted to climb out of the bed and teased, "I guess I should let you get on with things in peace."

He blew out a breath and turned away to press his face into the pillow. "Sorry," he mumbled into the muffling feathers. "I'm so sorry." In spite of everything, a giggle bubbled up from his heart.

"Oh no," Elspeth insisted. She reached for something in her trunk, then appeared at the very edge of his vision, rushing for the door. "I understand. Men have…needs. Don't let me disturb you."

She pulled open the door, flew into the hall, then shut the door behind her. A muffled laugh followed.

Athos closed his eyes and did the only thing he could. He laughed at himself, laughed at the ridiculousness of getting caught doing the same thing that Hubert probably lived in terror of being caught at, and laughed because Elspeth was laughing with him. That last filled his heart and soul with a kind of bliss that he never saw coming. She hadn't screamed or scolded or been disgusted, she'd laughed. She'd understood.

He sighed and shook his head, rolling over gingerly and slipping out the clean side of the bed. He should have turned to her for release after all. As he walked carefully to the wash table to clean up, he vowed that next time he would.

Elspeth didn't say anything about the incident once he had cleaned up, dressed, stripped the bed, and headed downstairs, but she did grin and giggle the whole way through breakfast. They didn't really talk about anything. All they could do was sit there and snort over their sausages, well aware of the implicit joke in what they were eating. It wasn't until Elspeth hurried upstairs to dress for church that he realized they'd passed the morning together happy and silly, even though the children weren't there.

The sobering truth that the children weren't there grew even more meaningful when they arrived at church for Sunday services only to find that neither the children nor the Bonneville family were in attendance.

"I would have expected them to at least bring the children to church," Athos whispered to Elspeth as they took their seats, waiting for the service to start.

"Perhaps they decided to conduct their own services at the ranch?" Elspeth suggested.

Athos shook his head. "I seriously doubt it. Bonneville is the sort who goes to church to be seen, not to worship."

That thought and the absence of his family—well, except for Elspeth—stuck with Athos through the entire sermon, making it impossible for him to concentrate. He was a basket of nerves by the time Rev. Pickering finished and adjourned the congregation to the potluck that waited for them under the tent outside.

The very same tent where his youngest angels had rammed into the Bonneville sisters all those weeks ago, setting the horrible wheels in motion that they were now dealing with. If he had just been a little more contentious of his children. If he had only kept a closer eye on them.

"I can't just stand here socializing when my children need me," he blurted in the middle of a conversation with Pete and Josephine Evans and Libby and Mason Montrose. Whatever they were talking about came to an abrupt stop at his impatient statement. "We should go out there and demand to see them," he went on, turning to Elspeth.

"If that's what you want to do." Her eyes shown with

just the sort of enthusiasm he needed to see from his helpmate right about then.

"Then let's go." He smiled and reached for her hand.

"Uh, Athos, are you sure that's a good idea?" Pete asked, holding out an arm to stop Athos and Elspeth from rushing off.

Athos tripped on his first step away from the gathering and turned to blink at Pete. "Of course it's a good idea. The Bonnevilles shouldn't have gotten involved in the first place."

Pete and Mason exchanged looks, but it was Libby who said, "Are you certain you shouldn't ask Solomon about it first? From what he was telling us earlier, he has a plan for handling the situation."

Athos turned to search over the crowd gathered for the potluck. Elspeth searched too. "There he is." She pointed across the lawn to the church door where Solomon stood talking to Rev. Pickering.

The sensible thing to do would be to keep a cool head and talk to Solomon. But from the moment Athos had awakened that morning—definitely from that moment—nothing about his day had been sensible.

"I think we could get away with a quick little social call. Just to be sure the children are all right. They weren't at church, after all. Something could have happened. We have a reason to check up on them."

Elspeth raised her eyebrows, but her expression was as filled with determination as his heart was. "I trust your judgment."

He grinned, loving the sound of that. It made him feel competent. It made him feel…heroic.

"It'll just be a short, calm visit to be sure the kids are all right," he explained to Pete and Mason, in spite of their dubious looks. "We'll be back before the potluck is over."

As he led Elspeth away, walking fast enough to draw curious looks from friends and disapproving ones from the likes of Mrs. Plover and Mrs. Kline, Elspeth asked, "Will we be back before the potluck is over?"

Athos laughed. "I doubt it. It takes about half an hour to drive out to the Bonneville ranch."

He was right, even though he drove his wagon faster than he usually would. The roads to Bonneville's ranch were clear, and they hadn't had rain for the last few days, so they weren't muddy. His horse seemed as happy as they were to be able to run as fast as he wanted, and he was bolstered, knowing he was actually doing something instead of just sitting by.

Those confident feelings were squashed a little as they turned into the lane that led through the Bonneville land and up to the big house. They had barely gone ten yards when riders spaced all along the drive and the edge of the property started whooping and calling to each other. A few turned their horses and ran back to the big house.

"Looks like they were expecting us." Elspeth inched closer to him on the wagon's seat, resting a hand on his arm.

"Good," Athos answered. "Then they'll be expecting me to be as angry with them as I am."

Elspeth's anxious look shifted to an excited grin. Athos didn't say anything else as he continued to drive his wagon at a steady pace toward the house, but he did sit a little taller. He was in his Sunday best—although he still hadn't shaved, and if he was honest with himself, a haircut wouldn't be a bad idea—and with his mood the way it was, the Bonnevilles had better watch out.

"Get out! You are not welcome here." It was Mrs. Lyon that came charging down the steps of the

Bonneville's porch to intercept the wagon as they made the last turn into the formal yard. "You're not allowed to be here."

"Papa?" The hesitant call came from the porch around the side of the house. In no time, the kids all rushed around the corner from whatever they'd been doing at the back of the house. "Papa! Papa!"

Athos pulled his wagon to a stop and leapt down. He ran halfway across the yard to the edge of the porch where his kids were trying to escape before realizing that he should have helped Elspeth down. It didn't matter, she would understand. And at the moment, he was more concerned with Mrs. Lyon's four thugs and a pair of Bonneville's ranch hands who had leapt onto the porch to restrain the children.

"You keep your hands off of them," Athos shouted. "I'm only here for a visit."

"The court order does not allow you to visit," Mrs. Lyon insisted. She intercepted Athos halfway across the yard and shook a pointed finger at him. "You are in violation of the terms of the order I received to rescue these children. I demand you leave at once."

"Not until I make sure my babies are all right." He pushed past her, marching on to the porch. "Neva, Millie, are you all right?" he asked the two that had made it farthest along the edge of the porch rail.

"We want to come home, Papa," Geneva shouted.

"It's boring here," Millie followed.

That brought Athos up short. "Boring?" Boring was miles away from frightening or dangerous.

"Elspeth," Lael shouted, breaking away from the man who held him back and rushing to the edge of the porch.

Athos caught Geneva telling him, "Call her Lady Elspeth," as he pivoted to see Elspeth rushing toward him.

She rushed right up to his side, giving him another burst of confidence.

"What's going on here?" Elspeth demanded, as furious as he felt.

"That's what I would like to know," Mrs. Lyon snapped. "You are forbidden from setting foot on the Bonneville ranch. Leave now." This time she pointed her bony finger at Elspeth.

"Where in that rubbish piece of paper you thrust at me does it say a man is forbidden to make a call on his neighbors?" Elspeth asked with perfect, regal grace.

Mrs. Lyon's mouth dropped open, but it took her a moment to gather herself enough to say, "It's *implied*."

There wasn't time to pursue the argument further. The children had all started shouting, "Lady Elspeth! Lady Elspeth!" instead of "Papa!" Hubert broke away from Bonneville's ranch hand that held him, then turned and punched the man in the face.

"Hubert!" Athos barked, not sure if he should be scolding or congratulating his son.

Hubert leapt right over the edge of the porch, landing on the grass with a thud. He stood slowly and shook himself, then darted straight for Athos, throwing himself into Athos's arms. It was as much a shock to have his sixteen-year-old son hugging him as it was to watch him punch a grown man.

"Son, what are you doing?" he asked as he squeezed his boy tight.

"The Bonneville sisters are snobs," he whispered in a rush. "They haven't been able to stop talking about 'Lady Elspeth,' as if she's some princess or something. They don't dare do anything against us as long as we tell them Lady Elspeth wouldn't like it."

That was all he had the time to say. The ranch hand he'd hit—who now dripped blood from his nose—tore down from the porch and grabbed him by the back of his shirt. He yanked Hubert away, knocking him off his feet.

"Don't touch my son," Athos boomed. He surged forward and planted his own fist across the man's face.

The crack of bone followed, and the drip from the ranch hand's nose became a flood. Mrs. Lyon screamed, and even Elspeth gasped. On the porch, the children all burst into cheers of "Yay Papa! Papa will save us!"

"What's going on out here?" Vivian Bonneville's shrill voice preceded her and the rest of her sisters out onto the porch. They were all dressed in their Sunday best and kept a suspicious distance from the children and their guards.

"Eew! Blood!" Bebe shouted, slipping into hysterics.

Athos shook his aching hand out, knuckles bruised, and watched as Honoria rushed to catch Bebe as she swooned. The injured ranch hand doubled over, bleeding into the grass as a couple of his mates rushed forward to help.

"Get them inside," Mrs. Lyon shouted, her voice an octave higher than usual. Her sharp finger was now thrust at the children on the porch. "Get them away from this wicked display of violence and degradation."

"If a man attacks my son, you'd better believe I'm going to defend him," Athos shouted at her.

His declaration didn't do much, though. Mrs. Lyon looked at him as though he was a two-headed snake, skirted well out of his way as she side-stepped toward the house, then ran for the porch. Her men had already shooed all of the children but Hubert around the back side of the house. Hubert—who had fallen when the ranch hand yanked him—climbed to his feet, glaring murder at the other ranch hands. He balled his fists and started toward them.

"Hubert." Athos stopped him. "Your energy would be better served protecting your siblings."

Hubert jerked to face his father. For a moment he looked like he'd disobey him and start a fight anyhow. At what felt like the last minute, he changed his mind. "Just remember what I said about them." He darted a glance to the porch—where Vivian and Melinda were descending the stairs into the yard—then turned and jogged back to the house.

Everything had happened so fast that Athos had to take a second to remember what exactly Hubert *had* said. He remembered in a flash as Vivian squealed, "Lady Elspeth!"

A man was bleeding, eight children were being held hostage, and the property was swarming with thugs and toughs, but Vivian and Melinda wore pasted-on smiles as they glided across the yard to Elspeth.

"Lady Elspeth, it's such a pleasure to welcome you to our ranch," Vivian went on.

"We've been talking of nothing else since we were introduced yesterday," Melinda added.

Both women came to a shuddering halt in front of Elspeth and bobbed crude curtsies.

Elspeth's mouth sagged open. She darted a sideways look of disbelief to Athos. For their part, Vivian and Melinda didn't seem to recognize that Athos was even there, as if he was invisible.

"Who did you say your father was again?" Vivian asked.

"The Marquis of Southampton," Melinda hissed, smacking her sister's arm as though she'd committed a faux pas.

"Oh yes, of course." Vivian laughed in a way that made Athos's hair stand on end.

At last, Elspeth caught up to the absurdity of the situation. With one final sideways glance to Athos, her lips forming into an incredulous smirk, she executed a curtsy like Wyoming had likely never seen before.

"Yes, my father is Nigel Leonard, the Marquis of Southampton," she said, putting on a cool smile. "And my mother's father was the Earl of Northrup. His mother's father was the Earl of Clifford."

Vivian and Melinda gaped at her, their eyes glassy with admiration, their mouths open and gasping like trout.

"*My lady,*" Vivian said, breathless.

"Oh, you really have to come to tea now," Melinda said.

"Right now." Vivian regained her own stiff back and haughty demeanor.

"Yes, come to tea right now," Melinda agreed. "We can clear everyone else out of the house."

"Except for Cousin Rance," Vivian added.

Melinda's cheeks pinked. "Oh, right. *Cousin Rance* can stay." She shot her sister a teasing sideways look.

Vivian smacked Melinda's arm in a gesture that Athos supposed was subtle.

Elspeth's lips twitched and her eyes sparkled. She looked fully at Athos as if asking him what on earth was going on. In spite of everything, Athos had a hard time not laughing. And still the Bonneville sisters didn't so much as blink in his direction.

"I couldn't possibly come to tea today," Elspeth said. She was greeted by sighs of regret from Vivian and Melinda. "But I could come later in the week." She peeked at Athos.

Athos nodded. Hubert's secret flashed to his mind. The Bonneville sisters wouldn't raise a hand against the kids if they thought Elspeth would disapprove. And chances were that if Elspeth came to visit on her own, she could say or do or discover anything she wanted to.

His heart swelled near to bursting in his chest, and he gave his wife a subtle nod.

"Tomorrow," Melinda gasped. "Yes, we'll be able to prepare ever so much better if you come tomorrow."

"Tuesday," Elspeth said, chin tilted up.

Athos struggled not to laugh. His beautiful, charming wife had the situation and the Bonneville sisters completely in her pocket.

"Yes, Tuesday," Vivian agreed. "By Tuesday I might have some happy news to share."

She peeked over her shoulder, beaming and wiggling her fingers at a man Athos didn't recognize who had stepped out onto the porch to see what was going on. Melinda snorted. Vivian gave her another not-so-subtle whack on her arm.

"Ow," Melinda whined, rubbing her arm.

"If you will excuse us," Athos interrupted, "I think it's about time we went home."

Vivian and Melinda turned to him as though just noticing he was there…and just noticing that he was a half-dead, rabid possum.

"Yes, it is about time you got off our property," Vivian said with a sniff.

"It's a shame what a woman…a *lady*…has to do to survive in this wretched world, isn't it?" Melinda added for Elspeth.

Elspeth's brow lifted. She balled her hands into fists the same way Hubert had. Athos reached for her arm, looping it in his, and said, "Good day to you." He turned and tugged Elspeth away toward the wagon.

"I think one bloody nose is enough for this Sunday," he whispered to Elspeth.

Her fury cracked, and a giggle bubbled up from her lungs. "A pity. I was looking forward to spilling blood all over that awful frock the older one is wearing."

Athos chuckled. It was baffling to him that he could be in such good spirits when his children were locked inside the Bonneville house and a judge was on the way to determine if they would be taken from him forever. But after everything he'd seen and experienced in the last twenty-four hours, his heart was certain justice would prevail. It was becoming more and more certain of some other things too.

They reached the wagon, and he closed his hands around Elspeth's waist to help her up to the seat. A rush of inconvenient excitement pulsed through him. Sure, they had to focus on cleaning the house and weeding the garden once they got home, but perhaps they could find a few precious minutes or an hour for…other things.

"Wait!"

The cry popped him right out of his heating thoughts. Elspeth settled in the wagon seat and Athos turned to see who was calling after them.

"Wait!" The call was followed by a cough this time as Honoria ran across the yard toward them. Her sisters had returned to the porch where they were watching her with frowns.

"Honoria, get back here," Vivian snapped.

Honoria ignored them. As she reached the wagon, she clutched her chest and panted.

"Are you all right?" Athos reached for her to hold her up if she needed it.

Honoria shook her head, waving his hand away. "I'm not used to running, and this corset is too tight."

Athos's brow shot to his hairline.

"I just wanted to give you this." She reached into a pocket in her skirt and drew out a messily folded scrap of paper.

Athos took it and opened it. The paper was a hastily-scribbled note in Heather's handwriting. She must have written it very fast. Heather prided herself on her penmanship, and this letter was hardly better than chicken scratch. It simply read, "We love you Papa, and we are trying to be good. We want to come home. We know you will talk to the judge and tell him that you're the best papa in the entire world, and we know he will let us all come home to you. Let Elspeth know that we love her too."

A hard lump formed in Athos's throat, and his eyes stung. "Thank you," he croaked, smiling for Honoria.

Honoria blinked rapidly, as if she too struggled with tears. She glanced up to Elspeth, then at Athos. "I'll do whatever I can to make sure they're safe."

"Thank you," Elspeth said when words refused to come to Athos's lips.

Honoria pivoted to return to the house, but paused. "Do you want me to encourage them to…to give my sisters a hard time?"

There was enough of a spark of mischief in Honoria's eyes that Athos chuckled. "Only if it doesn't label them as hellions so that the judge sides with Mrs. Lyon."

"Right." Honoria nodded. "I know just the thing. And I'll bring you more notes when they write them."

"Thanks."

Honoria smiled, then picked up her skirts and ran back to the porch. As Athos walked around the wagon and climbed up, he heard Vivian and Melinda scolding

Honoria to high heaven. He shook his head. "Someone needs to swoop in and rescue that poor woman from her family."

Elspeth hummed in agreement. "Maybe we could help. But let's rescue the children first."

Chapter Nine

Elspeth didn't know what to make of the scene at the Bonneville ranch. It was like something out of a farcical novel. It had been years since she had given any consideration to her lineage, so to have the Bonneville sisters fawning all over her as if she was a member of the royal family was as baffling as it was uncomfortable. She should have set the sisters straight about who she was now and what she expected from her life. But the moment it had become apparent to her that she could milk the sisters' fascination with her family's title for all it was worth on Athos's behalf, she played along.

She would have done anything for Athos. That much came clear the moment he jumped down from the wagon and ran for the porch and his children, regardless of the dozen or so rough-looking ranch hands who had set their sights—and a few guns—on him. She wasn't sure if he'd noticed how much danger he'd been in. No, she was certain he hadn't had a clue. But she had seen the violent set of those men's shoulders and the complete disregard they had for anything but the orders they were given. It was a blessing that Mrs. Lyon had held them off when Athos punched one of Bonneville's men in retaliation for laying hands on Hubert.

She fully intended to tell Athos just how much danger he had been in, but as he pulled the wagon into the drive beside the house, there was already a small gathering of friends and neighbors there to visit.

The remainder of the day was taken up in being introduced to half of the rest of the town of Haskell. Elspeth was grateful to have so many people eager to greet her and wish her and Athos well, but if she was being honest with herself, she would have preferred to have Athos all to herself. She didn't even get that opportunity on Monday, as a whopping three trains were scheduled to pass through town at various points, starting early in the morning. Elspeth spent the day scrubbing the first floor of the house to a shine while Athos toiled away at the station from dawn 'til dusk.

"Are you certain you don't want me to stay home and help you get a start on the children's rooms today?" Elspeth asked midway through Tuesday morning, the day of her tea with the Bonneville sisters. She was already dressed in her Sunday clothes and had styled her hair fashionably to play into the image she needed to live up to.

"There's not much point," Athos laughed as he passed through each bedroom, filling his arms with books that belonged on the shelves downstairs. "There's a train coming in at noon. That'll have me busy for the rest of the afternoon."

"I suppose."

Elspeth leaned against the doorframe of Ivy and Heather's room, watching her husband for a moment. He already had ten books cradled in his left arm and was walking around the room—the least cluttered and chaotic of the four bedrooms—picking up more books and reading the spines. Here she was, about to head out into the enemy's lair in an effort to woo the Bonneville sisters into supporting Athos's cause—knowingly or unknowingly—and yet Athos himself didn't have the least bit of guile in him. His sandy-blond hair was in need of a trim and a brush. He'd finally found time to shave the day before, but a shadow of stubble covered his strong jaw now. He wore his usual uniform, one corner of his shirt untucked in the back. She didn't suppose he was the sort of man women looked twice at, but to her he was a treasure.

"What?" He blinked uncertainly when he caught her watching him. "Do I still have jam from my breakfast toast on my cheek? I swear, I don't know how it got all the way over there."

"No," Elspeth laughed, standing straighter. "I was just thinking about how lucky I am to have been matched with you."

He almost dropped his armful of books. "Me?" He chuckled. "I'm the one who got lucky."

"Oh, I don't think so." A zip of mischief fluttered around her gut, sinking lower. She swayed slowly closer to him, glancing up through her lashes at him, the way coquettes used to flirt with titled gentleman at balls. "Musketeers always end up with ladies, don't they?"

"I'm not a—"

She silenced his self-effacing protest with a gentle kiss on his lips. It was quick and with closed-lips, but when she pulled away, Athos's whole face had gone red and his eyes were wide with wonder.

"I'll tell you the full story of the Great Bonneville Tea once I return home," she vowed.

She turned and skipped out of the room, her heart light. The silence she left in her wake told her that Athos was frozen with surprise. That thought made her giggle all the way out to the stable.

Athos had offered to hitch the family horse, Wilber, to the wagon so that she could drive out to the Bonneville ranch, but Elspeth insisted on riding. Josephine Evans let her borrow a sidesaddle, and Freddy Chance from the livery came over to help secure it on Wilber's back. She hoped she cut the sort of figure that the Bonneville sisters would be impressed by as she mounted and started her journey through town, out along the ranch road, and on to the Bonneville ranch.

Whatever Elspeth expected after the scene at the ranch on Sunday, it was not the illustrious welcome she got. Just as on Sunday, guards had been placed around the drive and perimeter of the ranch. As she was wondering whether they were there because of the children or if Rex Bonneville routinely kept hordes of armed men at the edges of his property, two of them fired rifles in the air.

"Easy, boy." Elspeth leaned forward to soothe Wilber, who probably remembered the events of Sunday too well.

The gunshots alerted the family, and before Elspeth could reach the house, all four Bonneville sisters, Mrs. Lyon, and the man Elspeth had seen on the porch at the end of the mess on Sunday came flooding out of the house, across the porch, and, in the case of the sisters, onto the lawn.

"Lady Elspeth, you do us such an honor with your presence." Vivian rushed to the front to greet her as she tugged Wilber to a stop in the drive.

"Miss Bonneville." Elspeth nodded, going full-out and calling Vivian by the title that would have been used for the eldest sister if they were in London society. She should have returned the greeting with something equally polite, but frankly, she didn't feel like it.

"You're here, you're here!" Bebe clapped and bounced at the edge of the lawn, the flounces on her dress fluttering.

"It's such a pleasure to see you, my lady," Melinda said in her sweetest voice, then turned to one of the ranch hands and belted out, "Frisk! Get over here and take Lady Elspeth's horse," like a fishwife.

It was all Elspeth could do to keep a straight face. When the man Frisk reached her and offered a hand to help her dismount, she said, "That won't be necessary." Keeping her chin pointed up as much as she could, she unhooked her feet and slipped easily to the ground.

Vivian, Melinda, and Bebe cooed and smiled.

"So you're an accomplished horsewoman too?" Vivian asked. "You must come riding with me sometime."

Elspeth sent a sideways look to Honoria, who hung back from her sisters. Honoria pressed a hand to her smile, then hid it with a cough. That made it all the harder for Elspeth to keep a straight face. At least she had an ally in this farce.

Correction, she thought as she started toward the house with the sisters, several allies. One glance at the house, and she saw several small faces peeking mischievously out through upstairs windows.

"You'll have to excuse our feeble setting," Melinda said, walking with a strange, halting gait—as if she'd twisted her ankle recently—as they headed for the house. "We originally prepared for tea in the...in the drawing room," she emphasized the genteel term, "But it was filled with the strangest scent this morning."

"It smelled awful," Bebe clarified with a snort. "Like cow pies and dead fish at the same time."

Honoria coughed, covering half her face with both of her hands.

Elspeth swallowed the giggle that tried to push its way out of her lungs.

"It was the oddest thing," Vivian went on, jaw tight. "Especially coming hard on the heels of Melinda tripping over that marble on the stairs. Of course, I would have suspected those vagrant Strong devils—"

"But they've been locked in their room all day," Bebe rushed to finish. "And they don't have marbles."

Elspeth's smile dropped and her rage rose. "You've kept the children locked in a room?"

Out of the corner of her eye, she saw Honoria shake her head just as Melinda said, "Well what were we supposed to do? Mrs. Lyon says we're not allowed to let them get away." She didn't sound happy about the arrangement.

Elspeth snuck another glance at Honoria. Honoria pursed her lips, half rolling her eyes. She didn't seem to know how to communicate the full story of what Melinda's comment meant, though. At least not before they reached the porch.

"I just want you to know that I'm against this in every way." Mrs. Lyon bit out her words, crossing her arms. "Just because she's a lady of some sort doesn't make her any less a culpable party in this case."

A twist of worry filled Elspeth's chest. It was quickly banished as Vivian brushed the woman's comment aside with, "The Bonneville family will always have a place at their house for anyone as *genteel* as Lady Elspeth."

"I don't see that she's—"

"Lady Elspeth," Vivian cut Mrs. Lyon off, a hard edge to her voice. She sent the woman a look as sharp as a dagger, then put on a cloying smile. "I'd like you to meet someone very special to me."

Vivian glided further along the porch to the side of the man who Elspeth didn't know. Melinda and Bebe grinned and snickered, taking up places where they could watch both Vivian's and Elspeth's reactions. Honoria stayed closer to Elspeth, her expression schooled to careful neutrality.

"So this is the fancy, titled noble you were telling me about, Viv?" The man elbowed Vivian, leering in Elspeth's direction. He had a similar, blond coloring to the Bonneville sisters and the same wolfish look in his eyes.

Vivian's smile faltered, but she forced it back again and took the man's arm. "Lady Elspeth, I'd like you to meet our cousin, Rance Bonneville." With a simpering sigh, she added, "My fiancé."

Elspeth swallowed her initial impulse to laugh out loud. She extended a hand to the man. "It is a pleasure to meet you, Mr. Bonneville."

"We're third cousins, in case you were wondering." Rance took a big step forward, wrenching out of Vivian's grasp. He took Elspeth's hand and kissed her knuckles with fat, wet lips. A chill passed down Elspeth's spine. It only got worse when Rance looked up and winked. "Cousin Rex needed a foreman for his ranch here. He couldn't trust none of these knuckleheads to do the job—" He darted a look to a few of the ranch hands who had wandered close to see what was going on. "—so he sent back to Kentucky for me."

"Now, now, Rance." Vivian's laugh was brittle enough to shatter. "Remember, we've been working on your grammar. Papa couldn't trust *any* of these ranch hands, not *none*."

"Yeah, whatever, Viv." Rance straightened and

tugged at the bottom of his jacket. "She's right. I gotta learn how to speak more like a ranch owner, since I'll be inheriting Cousin Rex's land one day."

"*I'll* be inheriting the ranch," Vivian clarified, her smile fading.

"Yeah, and I'm marrying you." Rance shrugged.

Bebe snorted. Mrs. Lyon rolled her eyes as if she had reached the end of her meager supply of patience.

"Why don't we adjourn to the back porch where tea is set up?" Melinda suggested, leading the way.

"Actually—" Elspeth stopped them all before they could take two steps. "—I was hoping to see the children."

"We're right here," a muffled call came from the other side of a window not three feet from where Elspeth stood. Tapping followed, and Elspeth pivoted to find Thomas, Geneva, and Lael peeking out through the curtains.

A moment later, they pulled back—whether by force or of their own volition, Elspeth couldn't tell.

"Those children are supposed to be upstairs," Mrs. Lyon barked. She shook her head and marched around the corner of the house.

"I'd better see what this is all about." Honoria sent a meaningful glance to Elspeth then followed.

Three seconds after she disappeared around the corner, there was a crash.

"Was that china?" Bebe yelped. "That sounded like china!"

"If those miscreants did anything to my rosebud china set," Melinda began, but didn't finish. She and Bebe tore off, skirts flying.

Vivian laughed nervously. "Right this way."

She attempted to escort Elspeth around the corner to where a round table had been set up in a wider section of the back porch. As she opened her mouth to speak, there was another crash, and Melinda cried out, "Vivian!"

Vivian flushed scarlet. "I'd better see what that is. Rance, please make our guest comfortable." She skittered off, jumping inside of the house, the door slamming behind her. A moment later, she screamed.

Elspeth stayed where she was, wondering what sort of mischief was going on inside, wondering whether the children were involved. Well, of course they were involved. The question was whether they were acting on their own or whether Honoria was helping things.

Rance cleared his throat. He sidled closer to Elspeth, running a finger down the arm of her dress. "You know, I hear that divorces are easy to get these days."

"What?" Elspeth backed away.

Rance took that as an invitation to chase her. "Viv and her sisters can't talk about nothing else. They think it's a crying shame that a lady like you should be chained to a fool like Athos Strong."

"I beg your pardon?" She attempted to flee to the far side of the table, shifting a chair into her wake with her toe so that Rance couldn't follow.

The impediment only made the hunger in Rance's eyes flash. "I've never met the guy myself," he went on. "Viv says he's a pill, though. And a slob. They've been hatching all sorts of schemes to get you out of that unfortunate marriage."

He carefully tucked the chair Elspeth had moved back into the table, then continued stalking her.

"Athos is a good man," she insisted, twisting this way and that to figure out how she could escape. The porch on the other side of the house was blocked by an arrangement of outdoor furniture. She was forced to back against the railing. The only way out would be to go up and over.

"Melinda seems to think you could probably get an annulment," Rance went on, slower now that he knew he had her cornered. "I'm not so sure. You have the look of a woman who wouldn't say no to a roll in the hay."

"Mr. Bonneville," Elspeth snapped, changing tactics and facing him with a straight back and an indignant expression. "It may be common to speak to women in such a low manner in Kentucky, but I can assure you, it is not welcome in Wyoming."

Rance chuckled, stalking closer still. "Oh, I think you like it."

"What on *earth* would give you that impression?"

He shrugged. "I've never had any complaints before." He leaned closer. "I'm considered quiet the catch where I'm from."

Elspeth pressed her backside all the way against the railing to avoid touching the man, She glanced over her shoulder, calculating how likely she was to break her ankle if she jumped.

"So why don't we just go ahead and get you annulled, and I'll throw Cousin Viv over, and then the two of us can do each other the justice we deserve." He pressed in, eyes closed, lips pursed.

"Sir, you must be out of your mind to assume that I would even begin to consider something so vile as—"

"What's going on out here?" Vivian demanded from the doorway.

Rance whipped around, reaching for the nearest chair and pulling it out without so much as breaking a sweat. "I was just making sure Lady Elspeth had the best place at the table," he said. "Oh, and she had a spider on her shoulder. I flicked it away."

Vivian's expression vaulted through about ten kinds of emotions before settling into an overly-sweet smile.

"You're so considerate, my dear. Isn't he considerate?" She marched over to Rance and grabbed his arm, yanking him away from Elspeth and around the table.

Elspeth never thought she'd be so grateful for any action on Vivian Bonneville's part. Melinda and Bebe rushed back onto the porch a moment later, then Honoria behind them.

"It was nothing," Melinda laughed, crossing to sit with a plunk at the table. "Just an accident."

"Wind doesn't blow over vases on the far side of the room," Bebe said, crossing her arms.

"It was a strong wind," Honoria mumbled, taking a seat next to Elspeth as she too sat.

Bebe humphed, then demanded, "Move, Honoria. I want to sit next to Lady Elspeth."

"I—"

"No, I am going to sit next to Lady Elspeth," Vivian announced in her most regal voice. She dropped Rance's arm and swept around the table. "Get out of that chair, Honoria."

Elspeth's back went straight. "And what if I want to sit next to Miss Honoria?"

"No, it's all right," Honoria whispered, getting up and scooting to the side before anything more could become of it.

Vivian leapt into the chair as though they were playing a party game. Bebe pouted, then skipped all the way around the table to sit on Elspeth's other side. Elspeth made no complaint about that since Bebe shoved Rance out of the way and occupied the chair before he could. Rance gave up and circled back around the table to sit between Vivian and Melinda, leaving Honoria to take the seat beside Bebe. That left one open chair.

"Where's Mrs. Lyon?" Bebe asked, already reaching

for the teapot on the table. She started pouring a cup for herself.

"Bebe." Vivian huffed and rolled her eyes. "You're supposed to pour for our guest first."

"But I'm thirsty," Bebe protested.

"Pour!"

Elspeth jumped at Vivian's shouted command. Bebe spilled tea, her hands were shaking so much as she poured Elspeth's cup.

"Now, Lady Elspeth," Vivian said once they were all settled, with tea and cakes brought out by a harried-looking girl in plain clothes. "We want to talk to you about your future."

"My future?" Elspeth reached for a dainty lemon tart.

Across the table, Honoria shook her head slightly. Elspeth's hand paused over the plate of confections. She arched a brow. Honoria flicked her eyes to the side. Elspeth moved her hand over a raspberry tart instead. Honoria nodded, so Elspeth picked it up and transferred it to her plate. The whole exchange took place in less than three seconds.

"Your future," Melinda added.

"It seems to us as though you are in an indelicate situation," Vivian went on. She helped herself to the lemon tart, then took two more. "And by that I mean the unfortunate circumstances in which you came to Haskell."

"Yes," Melinda said, taking a lemon tart and a raspberry one. "Of course, we understand that even a lady of your breeding and…and fortune, I'm sure, can fall on hard times. I suppose Hurst Home was a necessary evil."

"As was your marriage to that reprobate, Athos Strong." Vivian bit into her lemon tart as she finished. Her face scrunched in shock.

"What does my marriage have to do with anything?"

Trying her best not to look at Honoria—she would have burst into laughter for sure if they accidentally caught each other's eyes—she took a delicate bite of her raspberry tart. Melinda bit into her lemon one at the same time and made the same puckered, disgusted face as Vivian. Sensing the game, Elspeth proceeded to eat the rest of her tart as deliberately and politely as she could. Wincing and grimacing, Vivian and Melinda followed her lead, consuming their entire tarts. Honoria hid her expression behind her teacup. What had been put into the lemon tarts?

"Your marriage," Vivian began, but coughed. She snatched up her teacup and drained half of it in one gulp. She pursed her lips and shook her head, then took a breath. "Your marriage is an impediment that someone of your standing should not have to be saddled with."

"See?" Rance leaned back with a smug grin, crossing his arms.

"You have to get a divorce," Bebe blurted. She reached for a lemon tart, took a huge bite, then spit it out onto her plate. "Eew! What's wrong with that? It tastes like…it tastes like anise."

"Maria!" Vivian shouted at the door to the house. "Get your incompetent hide out here and take these disgusting tarts with you. What is wrong with you, you useless, immigrant scum?"

The back door opened, but instead of the servant from before, Mrs. Lyon stepped onto the porch. Ivy and Heather followed behind her. They were dressed in school clothes, their hair in perfect braids down their backs. Each wore expressions that were far too meek to be real.

"Girls." Elspeth jumped to her feet, rushing around the table to hug each of the twins.

Ivy and Heather hugged her enthusiastically, but then stepped back, hands clasped in front of them, and bobbed cute curtsies.

"We asked Mrs. Lyon if we could come down to help with tea," Ivy said, all innocence and sweetness in her hazel eyes—eyes very much like Athos's...when he was up to something.

"Yes," Heather agreed, turning to Vivian. "We've been ever so impressed with your kindness and hospitality, and we want nothing more than to help you out."

"I think it should be stated that I am against this," Mrs. Lyon said. She marched around to the empty chair at the table and sat. "You can pour my tea."

Elspeth balled her hands into fists, wanting nothing more than to throttle the woman.

"Yes, ma'am." Heather bobbed another curtsy, then rushed to find the teapot and pour a perfect cup of tea for Mrs. Lyon.

"Would you like cream and sugar?" Ivy asked with impeccable manners.

Mrs. Lyon smirked as though she was single-handedly responsible for the complete turn-around in the girls' attitudes. "Yes."

"Please, allow me." Ivy hurried to pour cream and sugar into Mrs. Lyon's cup.

The Bonneville sisters—all but Honoria—watched with wide eyes and mouths that sagged open.

"Well, those two *have* been kind of nice," Bebe admitted as Elspeth edged back to her seat. "They were only a few years behind me in school."

"Speaking of which." Elspeth pulled her chair into the table and sent piercing glances around the table to the sisters and Mrs. Lyon. "Why aren't the older children in school right now? As I understand it, they weren't in attendance yesterday as well."

The sisters sniffed, looking baffled and a little worried.

"It's the end of the school year anyhow," Melinda excused them. "No one does anything at the end of the school year."

"I was supposed to take a test," one of the boys shouted from inside the house.

Mrs. Lyon slammed her teacup down, chipping the saucer. "Who let them out of their room this time?" she hollered at the open back door. "I simply don't understand how the lock on that door keeps coming undone."

Thumping footsteps and giggles followed.

Elspeth arched an eyebrow at Mrs. Lyon. "I wonder what Judge Moss will have to say about the children's lack of school attendance this week. Especially considering, as I understand it, they had very good attendance while living with their father."

"And you know, Ivy and Heather are really quite tame," Honoria added, just above a whisper.

"Shut up, Honoria," Vivian snapped.

"Viv, is that how you talk to your sister?" Rance asked.

Everyone at the table seemed surprised to remember he was there. Vivian flushed pink and scowled. A moment later, she laughed. "Oh, Rance."

"If the older girls are well-behaved, it's got to be the influence we've had on them," Melinda said. She reached for the lemon tart on her plate, remembered the disaster of before, then carefully picked up the raspberry tart. She nibbled on the corner, and when it didn't produce any outrageous effects, bit into it.

"Yes, indeed," Elspeth agreed. Her heart raced as she tried to figure out how much to push things now or whether to wait until they were all in front of a judge to spring the trap. "Perhaps they should stay here even after the judge makes his pronouncement."

Mrs. Lyon snorted in derision. Rance curled his lip in a sneer. But to Elspeth's surprise, neither Vivian nor Melinda nor Bebe shouted out against the idea.

"I suppose young people can be shaped and molded," Vivian said. She picked up another tart from her plate, then grunted and put it down again. "Where is that idiot Maria? These tarts are poisoned."

"I'll take care of that for you, Miss Bonneville." Ivy rushed forward and removed Vivian's plate with a flattering smile.

"I'll get rid of this, and we'll fetch you something else," Heather said, reaching in to take the platter from the center of the table.

As soon as they had disappeared inside, Bebe said, "You know, those two always were nice. And Hubert isn't so bad either." She blushed and failed to hide a smile. "He's only two years younger than me, you know, and he's already sort of got a job at the train station."

"Shut up, Honoria," Vivian snapped. "I…I mean shut up, Bebe."

Across the table, Honoria rolled her eyes.

Elspeth's mouth twitched. She fell back on the best thing she knew to keep herself from laughing or giving up the game too soon. "We've had lovely weather since I arrived in Wyoming."

"Oh yes," Vivian rushed to agree. "Of course, the weather in Wyoming can be severe."

"I like the summers," Melinda added.

Just like that, they steered clear of anything dangerous or incendiary. The topic of the weather was followed by those of fashion, the upcoming centennial celebration, and Vivian's impending wedding. For the time being, Elspeth considered that she had accomplished her mission. With just a little prodding, she was convinced they would end up supporting Athos in the courtroom, whether they knew they were doing it or not.

Chapter Ten

Picking up clothes and toys and scrubbing away stains was a thousand times easier than clearing up old memories. Athos bent to gather the twin ragdolls Natalie had sewn for Geneva and Millicent from the corner where he'd found them under an old tablecloth. He straightened and held up the dolls, smiling with bitter-sweetness. Natalie had been pregnant with Thomas when she sewed the dolls especially for Neva and Millie. The girls had only been three at the time, and when they were presented with the homespun dolls, they hadn't been as excited about them as Natalie had hoped they would be. Her mother had just sent them expensive dolls with porcelain faces and hands from Hartford, and the tiny twins didn't think anything their mother could make would compare. But then, there was no accounting for the toys that children took a special fancy to.

He hugged the two ragdolls, wishing he could hug their owners, and stepped across the remaining piles of toys, clothes, and books to nestle the dolls safely on

Geneva's and Millicent's beds, beside the two fine, if faded, porcelain dolls.

"Don't you worry, your mommies will be home soon."

He took a step back from the beds and studied the picture the dolls made. Two different kinds, plain and fancy, store-bought and heartfelt. He laughed. If that wasn't a metaphor for his marriage to Elspeth, he didn't know what was.

He went back to work, sorting the flotsam and jetsam strewn around the room into specific piles, listening for Elspeth to come home. The house was bad enough without the children in it, but without Elspeth too it seemed like someone else's house entirely. He wondered what she was doing right then, wondered if the Bonneville sisters would be as impressed with the sight of her as he had been when she stepped out that morning.

He paused in his work, arms filled with clothes he'd forgotten the girls owned because they hadn't been put with the rest of the laundry for weeks. Elspeth had kissed him that morning. Bold as brass. She'd stepped right up to him when he was in the middle of a sentence and pressed her sweet lips to his. Even now, he was stunned to stillness at her action. She'd kissed him when she didn't have to, her lithe body swaying toward his. What a joy that had been.

The door opened and shut downstairs, and Elspeth called out, "Athos? I'm home."

Athos opened his eyes and took in a breath. He hadn't realized he'd shut his eyes to begin with. Heat flooded his face and he laughed at himself. "I'm up here," he replied. "But I'm about to come down."

Arms bundled with dirty clothes, he headed out to the hall and down the steps. Elspeth stood in the front entryway, removing her stylish hat with gloved hands. His heart skipped a beat. She was the most beautiful and elegant woman he'd ever seen, and by some crazy twist of fate, he'd married her.

"How was it?" He asked, trying to keep his awed reaction to the sight of her and the scent of lavender that filled the hall as she hung her hat on a peg by the door and removed her riding coat.

"It was everything you would imagine it would be," she answered, arching an eyebrow, barely able to contain a laugh. She only tried for a second before it came bursting out. As she tugged off her gloves, she said, "The sisters were horrible and conceited, as expected. All except Honoria, of course."

"I hope some nice man sees that woman's worth someday and whisks her away from her family," Athos said. He nodded down the hall, indicating that he was on his way to take the pile of clothes in his arms to the downstairs washroom.

"Why didn't you snap her up when you could?" Elspeth asked, following him.

"I…I never really thought about it. And now I wouldn't dare think about it. I'm married to you, and you're the only one for me."

His words caught up with him a moment too late and he winced as he crossed through the doorway into the washroom. What a silly, sentimental thing to say, especially when they'd known each other for less than a week. Even if they were married. What would she think of h—

"That's the sweetest thing anyone's ever said to me." Her words were a soft hush.

He dropped his load of clothes into an empty laundry basket then slowly turned to her. Elspeth held her gloves in front of her, head tilted down, gazing at him through lowered lashes. Her cheeks were pink, and her lips formed a perfect, kissable line.

He froze in place, even though his blood pumped through him. His heart felt as though it was swelling until it was too big for his chest. Other things threatened to start swelling too. He wanted to march boldly up to her and take her in his arms, like a hero in a storybook, like a musketeer.

He waited too long.

"I met the Bonneville's distant cousin, Rance Bonneville, while I was there," Elspeth went on with a smirk. The spell was broken.

"Rance? Don't think I've ever heard of him." He cleared his throat and skirted past Elspeth and into the hall, heading back up to the bedrooms.

"He was the man standing on the porch at the end of everything on Sunday. Apparently Bonneville brought him in from Kentucky to be the foreman on his ranch."

"Ah." Athos nodded. "I know he needed someone. Travis Montrose was going to take the job last year, but things fell through."

"Yes, well, if you ask me—or rather, if you ask Cousin Rance—he's there to manage more than just the ranch." She followed him upstairs, slipping into their bedroom for a moment to put away her gloves, then joining him in Geneva and Millicent's room.

"How so?"

Elspeth's lips twitched into a giggling grin. "He's engaged to Vivian Bonneville."

Although he was headed to the pile of toys in the corner to start putting them away, he stopped at the announcement and spun to face Elspeth. "No!"

"Yes." Elspeth laughed, crossing to join him near the pile and bending to gather some toys. "The wedding will be next month, apparently."

"Rex Bonneville actually found someone to marry Vivian." Athos shook his head. He contemplated the idea for a moment, then shook his head again and went to work putting away toys.

"The best part—or so Vivian kept insisting—is that she won't even need to change her name. Rance is Rance Bonneville, and after marriage, Vivian will still be Vivian Bonneville."

"I'm sure she will be," Athos laughed. "I'm not sure whether to pity poor Cousin Rance or to applaud him for his efforts."

Elspeth stepped over a stack of books to arrange a handful of doll furniture and clothes on the shelf beside one window. "Well, before you decide to make friends with Rance Bonneville, you should probably know that he suggested quite insistently to me that I should seek a divorce and marry him instead."

"What?" Athos fumbled the book he had bent to pick up. It slapped onto the floor with a bang. He'd kill the man first chance he got. That is, unless Elspeth actually wanted to divorce him and marry someone else.

A cold knot formed in the pit of his stomach.

Elspeth turned away from the shelf and bent for more toys, but paused at the sight of his face. "Don't worry." She rushed to reassure him. "I wouldn't dream of divorcing you for any man, let alone Cousin Rance. And you don't need to plot revenge for the insult. After what I saw, I think Vivian will be punishment enough."

She chuckled. The sound put him at ease by the slightest bit. Not enough to shake the moment of terror at the very suggestion she could walk away from him. Of course, he'd let her if she really wanted to, but...but he absolutely didn't want her to.

"The children are safe and as happy as can be," she went on, continuing to put away toys.

Athos forced himself to take a deep breath and focus on what really mattered. "I hate not having them here, where they belong."

"I know." They were hunched over the same, shrinking pile of toys, so she squeezed his arm. Warmth radiated through him from her touch. "They're not as miserable as I would have expected, though. I think Honoria is keeping them busy."

"Honoria?" The single word came out rough, and it wasn't even close to what he wanted to say. What he wanted to say was "Don't ever leave me. I need you. The children need you. Let me make love to you." He blinked and took a step back at the potency of his thoughts.

Elspeth's grin grew mysterious. "The children behaved like perfect angels. Ivy and Heather even helped serve tea. But it seems as though strange things have been occurring at the Bonneville ranch this week."

"Strange?" He picked up the books on the floor and began shelving them.

"Odd smells that no one can find the source of. Food that looks fine but tastes horrible when you bite into it. And Melinda told a long story about how there is a drip somewhere in her bedroom that kept her awake all night, nearly jumping out of her skin, but she can't figure out the source, since it hasn't rained in days and she doesn't think the roof leaks. She managed to trip on a marble that mysteriously appeared on the stairs this morning too."

"And you think the children have something to do with it?"

"I know the children have something to do with it. Honoria told me as much when we had thirty seconds to ourselves." She let out a deliciously mischievous giggle and sent a wicked look his way.

That look sent fire through his blood like few things ever had before.

"So they're enjoying their vacation after all." He forced himself to turn back to the bookshelf so that he wouldn't scare the stuffing out of her with the potency of how badly he wanted her right then.

"Enough." Elspeth scooped up the last of the toys from the floor and moved to arrange them on the other shelf. "I think they want to come home, though. Of course they do."

Before he could answer, there was a short cranking noise, followed by the tinkling strains of a music box. A wash of glittering memories swept through Athos. He stood and turned to find Elspeth smiling at blue, lacquered box.

"I haven't heard that song in ages," he said, shoulders relaxing.

"It's lovely." Elspeth gave the music box a few more winds. "We used to dance to this tune in London."

"I remember dancing to it too when I was young." The floor was completely clear for a change, so he crossed over to where Elspeth was smiling at the box. "Would you care to have this dance?" he asked with a short bow.

Elspeth glanced up, a look of pure delight coming to her bright eyes. She gave the music box a few more winds, then set it on the top of the shelf. "Why yes, sir, I would." She executed a perfect curtsy.

Deep, old joy and dazzling new happiness pulsed through Athos as he took Elspeth in his arms the way he had many a dance partner in his much younger years. He glided easily into the steps of a waltz, whisking Elspeth around the decluttered room.

"I haven't danced in years," he sighed, holding her closer.

"You're very good at it," she answered, surprise in her voice and expression.

He laughed. "You didn't think a tired, old stationmaster like me had it in him, did you?"

"I didn't say that." Her answering grin was both bashful and pleased.

"I used to love dancing." The statement swelled up through him with an unmanly burst of emotion. "Some of my friends scoffed that it was a stupid waste of time, but I used to argue that it was the perfect way to spend an evening with the ladies."

She laughed. "So you were a lady's man when you were young, were you?"

"No." He chuckled, stepping her through a turn. "Well, I suppose I would have been if I was one of those tall, handsome, dandy sorts."

"Who said you weren't?" She blinked, seeming genuinely surprised.

"It's obvious, isn't it?" Modesty urged him to lower his head, but a deeper sort of longing kept his shoulders squared and his eyes fixed on her beautiful smile.

"Not at all," she argued. "And if I had been a young lady at those long-ago balls, I would have scandalized every meddling mama in the room by standing up with you as many times as I could get away with."

He beamed from ear to ear at the thought. "We didn't have rules about how many times a couple could dance together back in those days. Then again, I always felt responsible for making sure the women that other men snubbed got at least one dance."

Her expression transformed before him from simply smiling to nearly weeping. And yet, her eyes shone with happiness.

"What? Did I say something wrong?"

"You danced with the wallflowers." Her voice was soft enough to be a whisper.

"They were more interesting anyhow." He shrugged. Her arms shifted as their waltz continued, embracing him more closely. Their steps became smaller and they turned in a tighter circle. His heart beat faster, but he wasn't sure why. "I...I always thought that that's what a musketeer would do," he said, intending to tease himself. "A hero should always show as much nobility of character to the less sought-after girls as to the popular ones, because every woman has the heart of a heroine beating inside of her."

"Oh, Athos!" She stopped dancing. The music had stopped playing. He thought maybe it had stopped playing several minutes ago and neither of them had noticed. "Athos, you are the most wonderful, heroic man I've ever met."

Her words surprised him, but not as much as the kiss that followed. She circled her arms fully around him, pulling him close so that she could press her lips to his. She didn't seem satisfied with just that. Her lips parted against his and her tongue brushed against the seam of his closed mouth. It didn't stay closed for long, though, and he didn't remain a passive partner in the kiss. Desire surged through him and he opened his mouth to take charge of their kiss. He sighed with longing, pressing her against him, not caring that she could feel the sudden insistence of how badly he wanted her pressing against her hip. In fact, he wanted her to feel that. He wanted her to feel what she did to him. He wanted her.

*   *   *

She wasn't going to let him find an excuse not to consummate their marriage or chicken out, like she suspected he had done at least once before. Elspeth's body was on fire, the ache in her heart furious, the need in her core desperate. She knew what she wanted from him, knew how to make sure that desire was fulfilled.

"Take me to bed, Athos," she whispered, nipping at his earlobe as she did. "Take me to bed right now." She lowered her grasping hands to tug the hem of his shirt out of his trousers, to let him know she meant what she said.

For a brief moment she pulled back, staring into his eyes. They were wide with disbelief. A moment later they flashed with a desire that was at least equal to her own.

He slanted his mouth possessively over hers in a kiss that took her by surprise. A scintillating hum rose up from his chest as his tongue danced with hers. He smoothed a hand down her back, reaching lower to grab a handful of her backside. He managed to find just the right angle to squeeze her even with the copious fabric of her bustle. He knew exactly how to spread his hand across her thigh and coax her to lift her leg to his hip, just how to support her so that she wouldn't lose her balance, and just how to grind against her to send a jolt of pleasure through her core. She gasped as she realized that, in fact, Athos knew exactly how to make her body sing.

He took that even further by lifting her against him, balancing her in his strong arms as she wrapped her legs around him. He took a few steps only, pressing her up against the wall next to the open doorway leading to the hall. His hips pinned her and he moved his hands swiftly up to undo the row of buttons that ran from her high collar down the front of her dress. The mad thought hit her that she should help him, but all she could do was grip the wall behind her, trying to find some purchase.

At last, he managed to completely unbutton her bodice, then spread it open, pushing the top aside and partway down her arms. It exposed her shoulder, but also bound her arms more tightly to her side. The sensation was scintillating, especially when he leaned into kiss her neck and shoulders. Not just kiss either, lick, nip, and suckle as well. She pressed her head back against the wall and closed her eyes, sighing with pleasure...and he hadn't even touched anything truly sensitive yet.

That changed in a matter of seconds as he rained kisses down to the top of her breasts. She arched forward, feeling her nipples harden against the constraint of her corset and chemise. She wanted to feel his mouth and hands on her, imagined how amazing it would feel if he would rake his tongue across her sensitive flesh.

Some part of him must have heard her. He pulled back, breathing deeply, only to unhook the fastenings of her corset. His hips still held her fast against the wall, the pressure of his staff clear through the layers of fabric around her legs. Her arms might have been constricted, but as he worked her corset loose, she gathered up handful after handful of her skirts, tugging them higher and struggling to remove as many layers of barrier between their bodies as she could.

As soon as her corset was as loose as it could get in their current position, he tugged the ribbon holding the front of her chemise, then pushed it aside. He flicked the chemise straps off her shoulders, and with a swift tug pulled the entire top of her dress down several inches. Her arms were further trapped at her sides, but her breasts slipped free of all restrains. A longing cry escaped from her. The muscles of her core twitched in anticipation, the ache there reaching dizzying strength, and she arched her chest forward.

He took up her invitation with heated intensity, cupping both of her breasts in his large hands. She hadn't realized how large his hands were, with long, strong fingers, until they were surrounding her.

"So beautiful," he whispered, stroking his thumbs across her nipples.

Her core tightened with pleasure in response. She squeezed her thighs around him, and he pressed into her harder as a reward. She bit her lip over a pleading cry, wanting him so badly she could hardly bring herself to breathe.

He responded by hoisting her higher and bending forward to close his mouth around her right breast. As his tongue flicked her nipple, she felt a jolt of pleasure so intense that for a moment she thought she might climax. She'd never done such a thing simply from her lover suckling her breast before. Then again, she hadn't felt even a fraction of the passion, of the love, for Craig as she felt for Athos now. And Craig had used her, whereas Athos's every touch and movement fired her blood. She gasped outright as he raked his teeth gently across the hardened nub of her nipple.

"Athos." She breathed out his name as a plea and a prayer. She wanted to reach for him, to thread her fingers through his hair and encourage him to go on, but her arms were held fast by her sides. She continued to draw her skirts up inch by inch as much as possible, but the fabric was caught between the two of them.

He inched back, then blew on her wet, inflamed nipple. She gasped and shuddered and squirmed at the sudden shock of cold when the rest of her was burning.

"Let me help you." His voice was a liquid purr, sending even more tremors pulsing through her.

Holding her carefully, first with one arm, then the other, he worked her skirts up until they bunched around her waist with her bodice in front and hung loose in the back. One hand continued to search as soon as the barrier was removed, testing the cotton of her drawers, finding the split in the center, and delving inside. He raked his fingernails against the tender flesh of her thigh. She had never been so grateful for split drawers in her life.

Without a lick of hesitation, he trailed his fingers right up into the wet heat of her opening. She started to gasp, and then shouted outright as he plunged a finger inside of her. The move was so unexpected that again she thought her body would burst into completion. She was sure she would have if Athos had moved or stroked or caused any further friction at all, but he didn't. He stayed perfectly still as they were. The mad intimacy of his finger inside of her as she panted, chest heaving, and fought not to bear down on him to find her own pleasure was dizzying.

He leaned closer and whispered, "Do you want it?" so close that his breath tickled her ear.

She wanted his mouth on her breasts again. She wanted him to tickle her inner walls and rub his thumb across the hard, pulsing point of pleasure between her legs. He was so close to touching her there already. She wanted him naked above her, below her, behind her, it didn't matter. She wanted him to take her in every way possible, even the ones she hadn't particularly enjoyed before, all at the same time and then again in succession. She wanted everything and more."

"This isn't enough?" he murmured, teasing her

earlobe with his tongue. Even that simple gesture ratcheted up her pulse. "You want more?"

Her heart burst as though he had heard her most wicked thoughts. "Yes," she panted, digging her nails into the wallpaper behind her. It was the only motion she was capable of right then.

He withdrew his hand from her, and for a moment she sagged in disappointment. Only a moment, though. She felt his hand moving, felt him swivel his hips, and then seconds later the hot, flared tip of his staff pressed into the molten folds of her sex.

She barely had time to open her mouth in shock before he thrust into her. It was quick and hard, forceful, and yet infinitely tender at the same time. And he was large. She shouted out of pure, primal instinct, pleasure building in her so fast that she was certain she would lose her mind. She jerked her hips, bearing down on him in restless, frantic movement as he held her against the wall and thrust hard and fast, growling with deep, male abandon as he did. There was no way she could hold on, and with cries in time to each of his powerful thrusts, she broke apart, her core convulsing with blinding strength around him.

Even after her passion had spent itself, she was still alive and pulsing with need. He continued to thrust in her until with one uncontrollable movement he surged harder, calling out, "Elspeth," then began to slow to a stop.

He leaned into her, using the angle of his body as much as his muscle to keep them both upright, wedged against the wall. Elspeth couldn't have moved if she'd tried. All she could do was feel the heat and weight and strength of him. Above all, she was acutely aware that he was still inside of her. He touched his forehead to the wall beside her, breathing heavily. She turned her head to him and smiled, beamed from the center of her soul. In no way had she ever imagined their first time would be as sizzling or as unusual as this. And crazy as it felt, she still wanted more.

As soon as his breathing began to steady, he lifted his head enough to look in her eyes. Uncertainty shone in his eyes at first, but he must have seen the excitement and continued hunger in her. His hesitance vanished, replaced by a renewed flame, and he shifted so that he could kiss her. This kiss was ten times as searing as the first ones. It was the kiss of a lover. His hands slipped down to her breasts again, and this time when he pinned her to the wall with his hips, he was inside of her.

"All right," he panted, breaking their kiss only to press his forehead to hers. His hands continued to knead and tease and own her breasts. "This is what we're going to do."

She hummed to let him know that she was listening.

"I'm going to slide out of you and then I'm going to set you on your feet."

"Mmm hmm." She licked her lips, moving her hips enough to tease him.

"After that," he resumed, his voice thick with continued desire, "we're going to our own bedroom."

"We are?" She breathed deeply, her chest thrusting forward into his hands. His gaze darted down to the swell of her breasts, her nipples still firm and pink as he played with them.

"And then we're going to get completely naked, because I want to see all of you."

"There are a few things I want to get a look at too," she panted. If her hands were free, she would have reached for those things right then and there.

He groaned and stole a hot kiss before going on with his plan. "Then I want you on your back in our bed, where I intend to kiss my way from your lips to your breasts to your stomach to your treasure chest. And then I plan to pick your lock with my tongue until you come about three more times."

"Oh," she sighed, giggling and mewling at the same time. Her hips twitched, and if she wasn't mistaken, he jumped and tightened inside of her.

"And after that—" His voice dropped to a roguish rumble. "—I'm going to sink so deep inside of you and take you so completely that you'll cry with bliss and shout out my name."

"Dear heavens, yes," she moaned, hips working as if she wanted to start right then.

"And then," he whispered, so sultry that she held her body rigid in anticipation.

"Yes?" she panted when he didn't go on.

"And then," he brushed his lips over hers, then kissed her with enough passion to draw her soul up from the deepest part of her. "And then you'll probably end up pregnant with triplets."

She burst into laughter, but it was a kind of silky, sensual laughter that she'd never felt before. He was so…Athos. So absolutely perfect in such wildly unexpected ways, and so devastatingly sweet at the same time.

"I tell you truly, husband of mine," she murmured, squeezing her inner muscles to hold him and surging forward to nip at his lips. "There are things I want you to do to me right now that I doubt the Bonneville sisters have the slightest inclination of."

"Naughty things?" He chuckled, the sparkle in his eyes equal parts humor, lust, and…and love.

"Very naughty things," she whimpered, exaggerating her already raging desire for him.

"I'm good at naughty things." He began to move subtly inside of her, hardening once more. "You have no idea how good at them I am."

"Are you?" She feigned doubt, moving in time with his thrusts, the pressure in her core growing all over again.

"Eight children don't conceive themselves," he said.

Elspeth burst into laughter a second time. Using her back against the wall to keep her dress in place, she wriggled her arms free of her sleeves and threw them around his neck. She pulled him closer, pivoting her hips against him as she drank her fill of his kisses. He responded enthusiastically, groaning and lightly pinching her nipples.

All of a sudden, he stopped. "Wait, wait. We're supposed to be moving to our bedroom, getting naked, and doing the rest of this in bed."

"Then let's get started," she purred. "Especially with the naked part. Because I want to be able to dig my nails into your back while you're inside me next time."

He answered with a groaning sigh and withdrew, easing her to her feet. She intended to make him sigh like that much more and much louder in the near future. He took her hand, and together they fled down the hall to their own room.

Chapter Eleven

Once upon a time, he had dreamed of being a hero. Wide-eyed, dreamy Athos would grow up to be Athos the Musketeer, Athos the rescuer of damsels in distress, Athos the noble warrior. How could he have forgotten those dreams? How could he have lost sight of the man he'd wanted to be, the man he was?

He was a man. The fact that he was realizing it, that it was something he needed to realize at all, left him chuckling and shaking his head as he lay in bed with Elspeth the next morning. He was stretched out on his back, limbs heavy with lack of sleep and exertion like they hadn't seen in a while. Elspeth curled against his side, an arm and a leg thrown over him. Her breathing was still deep and regular. As it should be. They'd worn themselves out yesterday, and worn themselves out again that night. And again.

He laughed at the thought and stroked his fingertips along Elspeth's arm. Did it make him some sort of a cad to be so proud of the pleasure he'd given her over hours the day and night before? She'd made no secret of her enjoyment. In fact, there had been a moment or two where he was worried Pete or Josephine Evans would come knocking on the door, telling them to keep it down. That thought raised more laughter in him. Really, why should he be ashamed of the two of them enjoying each other so thoroughly? They were husband and wife. They were in their honeymoon period. And clearly their levels of interest and taste for certain things matched. Far better than his and Natalie's had, no matter how hard he'd tried to do right by her.

The sigh he heaved as the last thought hit him was enough to shake Elspeth out of her slumber. She stretched against his side, sending a ripple of desire through him. Would he stop reacting so strongly to her someday the way he had with Natalie, the way she had with him?

No. Certainty filled his soul. No he wouldn't.

"You're too alert for someone who just woke up," Elspeth mumbled, then pressed a series of quick kisses over his heart.

"I didn't just wake up," he told her, grinning from ear to ear.

"Then why are you still in bed?" She shifted to prop herself up on one arm, studying him with sleepy eyes and a hazy smile.

Athos twisted to his side, fitting himself against her. He brushed a stray lock of hair back from her temple and kissed her softly. "Why would I want to be anywhere else in the entire world than where you are?"

Her grin widened and spread, sparking her heavy-lidded eyes to full wakefulness. "Would it be completely mad and impulsive of me to declare that I love you when we haven't even known each other a week?" she asked, voice low and sultry.

"No crazier than me saying that I love you as if I've known you my entire life." He spread his hand across her back and tugged her closer for a kiss.

It would have been a longer, hotter kiss, but morning was not the best time for kissing. It would have been the best time for other things, but twinges of soreness in his back and legs and the barest hint of a wince from Elspeth when she moved were enough to convince him to put all that aside for later. It didn't help when her stomach rumbled as he was kissing her neck. They both burst into flurries of giggles at the sound.

"This is what happens when you skip supper." She gave him one more, quick kiss, then peeled herself away, rolling out of bed.

Athos watched her, feasting on the enticing curves of her body as she moved. "I could look at you like that all day," he said as she bent to open the lid of her trunk.

She laughed as she picked out clean clothes, then stood. "Yes, well, I've been told men like to look."

Of all things, her comment filled him with joy. "I *am* a man, aren't I." He propped himself on one elbow and drank in the sight of her.

Elspeth tossed her clothes on the far corner of the bed, then crawled across the rumpled sheets to kiss him. "Athos Strong, you are every inch a man."

His heart squeezed in his chest. His most manly organ pulsed. He kissed her back, then admitted. "I'd forgotten."

She inched back and blinked. "How can you forget something like that?"

"Children," he shrugged. "Responsibility. Age. The cares of the world. Loss."

Her expression melted to something to tender it punched holes in him. She kissed him once more, passionate in spite of the practicalities of morning breath, then told him, "Not anymore."

She met his eyes. Something was different there. It wasn't just him that had remembered something in the amazing hours they'd spent together. Gone was the overwhelmed, uncertain lady who didn't know her place in the world. Now she was a siren, a lover, a wife. At least, she was to him.

"If we both don't get out of this bed right now, get dressed, and start taking care of the everyday business of life," he said, voice gruff, "then we won't be able to get out of bed for the rest of the day."

"I think you're right." She giggled, scooting backward and rolling out of bed. She headed to the table, pouring water from the pitcher into the washbowl.

"Imagine what the judge would say if we missed the hearing because we were…" He coughed.

Elspeth laughed out loud, dripping water on the floor as she bathed. "Imagine what the Bonneville sisters would say."

"I'd rather not." Athos threw back the bedcovers with a horrified expression. He got up, conscious that once again he would need to wash sheets before remaking the bed, and opened the wardrobe at the side of the room, fishing for his robe. "I'll just bathe downstairs to avoid any further temptations that might upset the Bonneville sisters."

He left Elspeth giggling so hard that she had to pause in her bathing, and headed downstairs. It was easier to think about life in normal terms when he didn't have the scent of Elspeth all around him, the heat of her body so close, and the divine sight of her filling up his vision.

They crossed paths as she came downstairs, fully clothed, to start breakfast while he was heading up to dress. Mischief seized him, and he waited until she was just one step below him on the stairs before turning around, scooping her into his arms, lifting her to her toes and giving her a long, sizzling kiss. Then he left her laughing and red as he bolted upstairs to get dressed for the day.

His heart had never felt so light, even though the children were away at the Bonneville ranch. Maybe this *was* some sort of unwitting wedding present that the Bonnevilles were giving him and Elspeth. As he tugged on his trousers he was filled with absolute confidence that the judge would see exactly where the children belonged once he heard all sides of the story. How could it be any other way?

"I'm going to do the rest of that laundry today," Elspeth informed him as they shared a filling breakfast at the kitchen table. "Then I'm going to start scrubbing floors upstairs. And I'm going to weed that garden this afternoon if it's the last thing I ever do. I want this house looking spectacular when that judge gets here."

Athos smiled, heart warmed that she shared his thoughts about things in so many ways. That too was a new, wonderful feeling. It was so bolstering that before he could give it much thought, he said, "And I'm going to march straight over to Howard Haskell's office at the town hall before work this morning and ask that he give me a raise and hire an assistant for the station."

Elspeth stopped, a bite of eggs halfway to her mouth. "You are?" Her whole face lit with admiration.

"Yes." He nodded, planting his hands on the side of the table, then rising to his feet. "It's about time I said something. The station just keeps getting busier and busier as Haskell grows and more trains stop here. It's no longer good enough for me to take all the work on my own shoulders. It's time I did the responsible thing and ask for help."

Elspeth rose and skipped around the table to hug him. "Bravo, musketeer," she exclaimed, then kissed him square on the lips. "How could anyone deny you anything?"

Of all the questions that had been running through his head for the past several hours, that one was the most unexpected, but as he kissed Elspeth back, it reverberated in his gut. How could they? How could Howard and how could Judge Andrew Moss?

He helped Elspeth tidy up the breakfast things, then plunked his stationmaster hat on his head, kissed her one more time, then marched out the door, ready to take on Haskell, the Territory of Wyoming, and the world. It was no surprise to him that more than a few of his neighbors stopped and did a double-take as he walked past on his way to the town hall.

"What's gotten into him?" Jim Plover muttered to Silas Purdue as Athos walked past the foundry across from The Cattleman Hotel.

Athos ignored them, even when Silas snorted and said, "With a look like that, it's probably what *he's* gotten into, or who, if you know what I mean."

"Good morning, Athos," Theophilus Gunn called from the top of the hotel's stairs, sending a scolding look across to Jim and Silas to show he'd heard their disrespect. "How are Elspeth and the children?"

"Elspeth is wonderful," he replied. "And I intend to send Solomon out to the Bonneville ranch as my agent to make sure that the children are safe and happy." That came as a surprise to him when he heard himself speak, but it too was a brilliant idea. Rex Bonneville hates Solomon, but even he had to let a reputable agent check up on the children on his and Elspeth's behalf.

"A fine idea," Gunn seconded with a nod.

By the time Athos reached the town hall, he was brimming with energy and ideas. Howard kept office hours on Wednesday, and as usual, he left the door to his office open while he was there. It was early and few people were at the town hall, so Athos was able to walk straight in and up to Howard's desk.

"Ah! Athos! How are you on this fine morning?" Howard boomed in typical Howard style. He rose from his great, leather chair—something he was intensely proud of—and circled around his desk to pump Athos's hand in greeting.

It dawned on Athos that Howard Haskell was exactly the kind of man he'd always thought he would be: fearless, visionary, and always willing to help his neighbors in any way possible. Men like that wanted to see the same boldness in others, so Athos wouldn't disappoint him.

"I'm as well as I can be without my children," he began, taking off his hat and shaking Howard's hand firmly, "and possibly a bit happier than I should be."

"You just married one of those brides from Hurst Home, didn't you?" Howard winked.

"I did, and she is perfect in every way."

Howard laughed from deep in his belly and walked back to take a seat behind his desk, gesturing for Athos to sit in the chair across from him. "There's nothing like a beautiful, loving wife to make a man feel like a king."

"Or a musketeer." Athos sat.

Howard's brow flew up for a minute. "Oh, right. Your name. I always wondered about that." He grinned and leaned back in his chair. "It suits you. So what can I do for you today, my musketeer friend?"

"You can ask the railroad to give me a raise." Athos jumped straight to the issue at hand.

Howard barked out a laugh. "I like a man who cuts right to the point." He pinched his face in thought for a moment, then said. "Done!"

Athos blinked, his new swagger dropping to old disbelief and shock. "Done? You'll see about getting me a raise, just like that?"

"I'm surprised you haven't asked for one sooner, to be honest."

Athos shook his head. "I would have asked much sooner, but with work being so busy and all, I've been putting it off. I wouldn't want you to think I was complaining or that I'm not on top of things, and I wouldn't have presumed. I...I mean, you know how to run the town's business dealings. The railroad answers to you, and the station falls under your prevue."

"I only have so many eyes to keep track of things and hands to get things done," Howard explained with a shrug. "There's no question that you do an excellent job down there at the station. Truly top-notch. I'm sure I've told myself a hundred times in the last few years to review your yearly salary and make a recommendation to the railroad to add to it, but with one thing or another..."

"I should have said something," Athos said, half to himself. "I shouldn't have tried to shoulder the whole load myself all this time." He should have believed in himself more too, but after years of struggling to raise children and keep a wife who didn't love him happy...

He pushed the unhappy thought aside and sat straighter. "Which brings me to another point. I also want you to hire an assistant for the station," he went on.

"An assistant?" Howard tilted his head, expression turning thoughtful.

"There are more trains arriving in Haskell than ever before." Athos scooted to the edge of his chair to make the point. "The job has grown since I first took it, and…and so have I."

Howard raised his brows but said nothing.

Athos went on. "I have a large family, sir, and a new wife who I…" He let out a breath, a sudden swell of emotion overwhelming him. "I love her, sir. I know that we've only been married for days and it was all arranged by someone else, but God was looking out for both of us when he put Elspeth and I together. I knew almost from the start that we were a good partnership, but in these last few days, with the children taken away…well, it's just been the two of us. And they've been intense days of soul-searching. Elspeth has given me back something that I didn't even know I'd lost, and frankly, sir, I owe it to her to be able to spend as much time as possible with her and with my children, as soon as I get them back. I want us to be a family, and families need to spend time with each other to grow and thrive. I want you to hire an assistant for me so that I can give as much of myself to my family as I've given to my job and to this town for the last ten years."

He finished and took a breath, shocked that he'd poured out so much in one go. Howard steepled his fingers and watched him, a grin growing on his mischievous, old face.

"Athos Strong, do you know why I hired you above all the other applicants who applied for the position of stationmaster?" he asked.

"I…" Athos frowned. "I thought it was the railroad's decision to send me here."

"I told them I wanted to pick my stationmaster, so they sent me files on ten different men, complete with their service records. I picked you because your file contained glowing endorsement after glowing endorsement from supervisors who stated that you were conscientious, outgoing, and that you always went above and beyond what was required of you."

"I... Thank you?" He wasn't sure who to thank or how to thank them.

"Being married and raising children is hard. I've watched you do it for ten years now. I watched when Natalie died, and as your children grew older without a mother." Howard punctuated his remark with a compassionate smile. "You've risen to more challenges than you know, young man. And you're rising to them now."

"I...I'm only doing what my family needs me to do."

"Which is a damned sight more than some men would do." Howard shifted out of his contemplative posture and rapped the top of his desk. "You'll have your assistant. I'll ask the railroad for recommendations and let you look over them with me to choose someone."

"Thank you, sir." Athos sank back in his chair, overwhelmed.

"And you'll get your raise too. The railroad can pay you what they want, but I'll add my own bonus on top of that."

"Wow." Athos blew out a breath, running a hand through his hair. "Thank you, sir."

"And don't you worry about this mess with your children," Howard went on. "I know you'll prevail."

Scrubbing floors with muscles sore from certain other activities was not as easy as Elspeth anticipated. Washing laundry and hanging it on the line wasn't either. By the time afternoon rolled around and she knelt with gardening gloves and a trowel in the front garden, pulling up weeds, she was in enough pain to severely curtail the blissful mood she'd awoken in.

It helped to hear the piercing notes of a train whistle growing closer. Hearing that made her think of Athos, made her imagine all the things he was doing down at the station to get ready to greet the new arrival. Thinking of him made her smile through her nagging soreness.

"The garden is looking nice."

Elspeth straightened with a wince and turned to see her neighbor, Josephine, walking past on the other side of the picket fence, returning home from an errand, a full basket over her shoulder. A few of her other new neighbors looked as though they had been out shopping as well, Mrs. Plover and Mrs. Abernathy, wife of one of Haskell's two doctors.

"Thanks." She smiled at Josephine and pushed herself to her feet. "I'm trying to make everything look perfect for the business on Friday." She sent Josephine a significant look.

"It already looks much better," Josephine reassured her. "Piper will love it when she gets back this autumn. She has always done what she can with the garden, but she's had her hands full with those kids."

"Piper," Elspeth gasped. "Oh dear, it just now dawned on me. Does Piper expect to live with all of us when she comes back?" She'd known that was the arrangement when she agreed to marry Athos, but now, after all they'd shared, the idea of having another woman in the house with them was…unsettling.

"I'm suddenly wondering if Piper might be more comfortable striking out on her own," Josephine said, a sly grin on her face as she studied Elspeth.

"I—"

"I'm surprised that poor woman hasn't turned tail and run long before this," Mrs. Plover interrupted, as though she'd been a part of the conversation from the beginning.

"I beg your pardon?" Josephine snapped.

"Do you really think she'll come back from Connecticut at all?" Mrs. Abernathy sniffed. "That poor woman was a virtual slave to those horrible children."

"Excuse me." Elspeth rounded on the women, planting her hands on her hips in spite of the dirt on her gardening gloves. "The Strong children are wonderful, sweet things.

Both women snorted with laughter, shaking their heads and sneering.

"If you believe that," Mrs. Plover said, "you're as crazy as everyone says you are."

Elspeth's jaw dropped, but her anger was eclipsed by a sinking sense of dread. She knew the looks that the two women across the garden fence from her wore. They were the same sort of looks the wives and friends of the wives of the families she'd worked for—the families whose husbands had assumed she would provide more services than tutoring children—had given her. In the last few days, since Athos had come into her life, she hadn't given those women or that sense of worthlessness a second thought. She didn't want to now, but old habits died hard.

"Nobody is saying Elspeth is crazy," Josephine said, crossing her arms and giving both women hard looks. "You two, on the other hand…"

Mrs. Plover and Mrs. Abernathy shared a decidedly snooty glance.

"Maybe the people *you* associate yourself with aren't saying that," Mrs. Abernathy said.

"Anyone who would shackle herself to a booby like Athos Strong must be a little weak in the head," Mrs. Plover added.

In seconds, Elspeth was enraged enough to spit at the women. She held onto her temper by a thread. "If you think—"

"They don't." Josephine put a hand on Elspeth's arm to stop her from surging forward. She glared at the two, sour women. "Those two don't have enough sense between them to think anything at all."

"Why, I have never been so insulted," Mrs. Plover said. "Come along, Jill." She tugged at Mrs. Abernathy's sleeve. The two woman marched off, their noses in the air.

The confrontation was over, and an unsettling feeling of disappointment and worry rushed in as anger left Elspeth.

"Don't pay any attention to those two," Josephine said. She cocked her head to the side, then added, "Or Beata Kline, for that matter. Every town has its sour old biddies, and those three fill the role for Haskell."

Elspeth faced Josephine with a weak smile. "Thank you. I'm sure you're right. But after everything Athos and the children have gone through, I am ready to strangle anyone who would disparage them."

Josephine chuckled. "That makes two of us."

Josephine left her to go about her business, and Elspeth crouched to return to weeding. Anger had pushed the pain out of her thoughts for a moment, but it came back again as soon as she tried to squat. She didn't know whether to cry or laugh at the protest from her thighs, knowing how they had gotten so sore in the first place. She didn't know whether to laugh or cry over the fickle course of neighbors and reputations either. How long would it be until someone in town heard whispers about

Elspeth's past and how she'd come to be at Hurst Home—or in America—to begin with?

Those and other irritating thoughts stayed with her, building and building, until she pulled up a handful of difficult weeds and was stung by a bee on her wrist for her efforts. She wheeled back, hissing, "Ouch, ouch," and landed hard on her backside on the front walk with a shock of soreness. The irritating pain, the horrible neighbors, and the uncertainty of everything with the children and the future doubled back on her, and for all those reasons and no reason at all, she burst into tears.

"Elspeth? Elspeth!"

Suddenly, Athos was there. She hadn't heard him coming, but once second she was sitting on her sore backside, sucking the sting on her wrist, shedding pointless tears, and the next he was rushing around the garden fence and crouching by her side. He held a bouquet in one hand and a small box in the other, but pulled her into his arms all the same.

"Sweetheart, what's the matter?"

Her pointless tears flashed to equally absurd laughter. "I was stung by a bee. Can you believe it? With everything else that's going on, I'm weeping because I was stung by a bee." She circled her arms around his shoulders and rested her forehead against his neck.

"All right," he chuckled. "You're okay." He rocked back and sat with a thump, shifting her to sit in his arms.

Elspeth lifted her head and blinked around through tear-blurred eyes. She shook her head. "Athos, we're sitting on the path in the middle of the front yard. Any number of our neighbors could walk by and think we're out of our minds."

"I don't care. I like you in my arms this way." He

grinned like a beautiful fool, then kissed her. It was lovely and absurd at the same time.

"What are you doing home so early?" she asked when he finally kissed away her tears and let her go for a breath.

"Ah." A gleam filled his eyes and he helped her to her feet. "Howard Haskell accepted my request for a raise and an assistant."

"Oh, Athos, I'm so happy for you."

"Happy for us," he corrected her. "So I bought you these on the way home."

First he held out the bouquet. "For me?"

"Absolutely. I want to bring you flowers every day."

"You don't have to do that."

"I want to," he insisted.

She started to smell the flowers, then stopped and eyed them suspiciously. "There are no bees in them, I trust."

"They wouldn't dare," he insisted. "No one, no bee, would dare offend the lady of a musketeer."

Elspeth laughed out loud at that and went to hug him.

He stopped her, holding up a hand and taking a step back. "And to prove that you're the lady of a musketeer, I bought you this."

He held out the small box, opening it to reveal a simple wedding ring. It wasn't expensive or fancy, just a gold band with a rose vine etched onto the surface. Elspeth gasped as though it was the richest jewel in the Queen's crown.

"It's beautiful." Now she was crying in earnest.

Athos took her hand and slipped the ring on. "I feel like I should be asking a question before I put this ring on your finger."

"But the answer's already been given and then some," she finished his thought.

"Exactly." With the ring on her finger, he slipped the box back into his pocket, then drew her into his arms for a kiss that the neighbors really shouldn't see. Even that was simply perfect.

"Now all we need is the children home and life will be complete," he said, breaking their kiss.

"Two days," Elspeth sighed. "Two days and we can put this mess behind us."

"Do you believe I'll win this appeal, Elspeth?" he asked with enough seriousness and concern to send Elspeth's heart pounding with love and sympathy.

"Yes, of course I do, Athos." She kissed him lightly, then went on. "You are the best father a child could have and the best husband too."

"I've never been—"

"Well you are now," she cut him off, hugging him tight. "And on Friday the two of us are going to walk into that courtroom, tell the judge this has all been some sort of stupid mistake made by vengeful nobodies, and then we'll bring our family home."

Chapter Twelve

The flurry of activity that had surrounded Athos and Elspeth since the moment Elspeth stepped down from the train a week ago was suddenly transformed into an expectant hush as Friday dawned. Athos had had a hard time sleeping. His thoughts refused to settle throughout the night. What if the judge sided with the dreadful Mrs. Lyon and the Bonnevilles? What if his dear, sweet, amazing children were taken away permanently, split up, and placed in institutions, or worse, with families who didn't love them? What if he truly was a failure as a father?

"It will be all right," Elspeth spoke out of the blue as the first rays of morning sunlight peeked through the curtains. "Everything will go our way, I'm certain."

"Are you?" He lay on his back, but turned to face her now, holding her close against him. That skin-to-skin contact was the only thing keeping him sane right then.

Elspeth smiled. He could only just see it in the dim light, but it ignited his soul all the same. "Yes, I'm certain. The more I've come to know your friends here in Haskell, the more I'm seeing that if you hadn't just married me, if they didn't think it would be grand for the two of us to have some sort of a honeymoon, they all would have moved heaven and earth to make sure the children were back under this roof after one night."

He stared hard at her. "Are you certain you're certain?"

"Yes," she said with a peal of laughter. "How could you expect a man with Howard Haskell's power—a man who gave you a raise above what the railroad pays you and is hiring an assistant for you to boot—would not swoop in and write a new law to keep your children with you if he had to?"

Athos tilted his head in thought. "You know, you're right." He blinked and sought out Elspeth's eyes in the growing light. "I am going to win this hearing, aren't I?"

"Yes, dear." She brushed her fingertips along the side of his face, then combed them through his hair, sending arrows of longing straight through him.

Mischief bubbled up and he rolled Elspeth to her back. "In that case, if the children are going to be home by this afternoon, we'd better make the best of the time we have alone."

He kissed her, hesitantly at first, but when she responded with enthusiasm, squirming beneath him to fit her hips against his and draw her knees up on either side of his thighs, with deeper passion.

"I may never get over how responsive you are," he whispered as he moved on to kissing her cheek, the tender spot where her jaw met her neck, the line of her throat.

"I surprise even myself," she teased, tracing her nails up the small of his back. The sensation fired his blood hotter, beginning the first stages of the delicious rush that would end with both of them in bliss.

"How can you be surprised at yourself when you're so free and open with me?" He shifted so that he could continue the downward path of his kisses, savoring the heat and tang of her skin as he made his way across her shoulder and collarbone to her breast.

She drew in a breath as he teased her nipple with his teeth, then suckled her, stroking her to tautness with his tongue. A moment of hesitation passed, and she said, "I was never like this with him."

Athos lifted himself above her, gazing down at the regret in her eyes that marred the haze of passion around her. "You were young," he said, almost a whisper. "And excited. And then probably a little terrified."

She swallowed and blinked as if fighting tears, then nodded.

"So was I," he confessed. "With Natalie. But that's all in the past, for both of us. And I'm grateful to her for teaching me what I needed to know for when you came along." He narrowed his eyes and went on with, "I suppose I should be grateful to *him* for teaching you what you needed to know and doing away with the whole fear part of making love before I came along."

Elspeth's sorrow turned into a fond laugh, and she pulled him close for a kiss. "All right. I suppose I should be grateful to him too. Because I feel nothing but the most ardent and scandalous desire for you."

It was all she needed to say to pulverize any lingering doubt he had. He kissed her lips with reckless abandon, then continued with his exploration of her breasts. She had magnificent breasts, round and full without being too much. A guilty, impish part of him wanted to take them out and play with them almost every time he noticed their fullness through her clothes. He supposed that was normal, but that part of him had been dormant for so long that the sensation was new once again.

He scooped one breast into his hand and lightly pinched her nipple as he suckled and teased the other one. Elspeth gasped and jerked her hips. "Oh Athos, if you continue that way I'll finish long before you."

He chuckled. "Then you'll have time to work your way up to another explosion by the time I'm ready."

She laughed, but that laughter turned into something far more sensual as he slid one hand down her stomach to delve into her curls. She was delightfully wet already, and as he stroked her nubbin, her cries became more frantic.

"Athos," she sighed, arching into his touch.

He hummed with pride and arousal at the pleasure he knew he was giving her. He sought to double it by bending down to lave her breast with the flat of his tongue. If he could have, he would have drawn her pleasure out for hours, teaching her all the little tricks he'd picked up over the years until she was sated. But that morning, time wasn't on their side, and as much as he wanted to test the limits of his endurance, there were other things that needed their consideration.

Right after they finished soaring to heaven and back.

"I love you, Elspeth," he whispered and increased the intensity of his fingers' work.

"I love you too, Ath—ohh!" She came apart halfway through his name, her body throbbing with completion.

A deep, deep surge of affection filled him, and he moved to slide inside of her so that he could feel her body's response. The hot, powerful squeezing around him was so beautiful that it drew every last bit of his focus. All he could imagine was the two of them joined that way, him working not to move too furiously until her tremors subsided so that he could feel them to the end, in all their glory.

Then he began to thrust in earnest, the friction and pull of her driving him past all rational thought. It wasn't just the sheath of her tight around him, it was her legs wrapping around him, her arms embracing him, her soul-deep cries of longing and love, her whole being surrounding him and keeping him safe. He could be her champion for the rest of his days, but she would forever be the keeper of his heart.

The potent rush of orgasm sped through him, gathering heat and energy from his spine to his thighs and barreling through his groin with unbelievable pleasure. He cried out as his life itself burst through him and into her, uniting them beyond what any vows could accomplish. He wished that moment of perfect unity could last forever, that they could float together in heady abandon forever, but already the feeling was subsiding, leaving him with a sense that everything with the world was absolutely perfect.

"My beautiful wife," he sighed, relaxing to the side so they could both catch their breath.

"My valiant husband," she purred, resting her hand over his heart.

He fell asleep again, which was shameless, considering the importance of the day. When he awoke, Elspeth was gone. The sounds of breakfast being prepared downstairs and the scent of bacon reassured him that all was well. He took a moment to lay there with a broad grin on his face, wondering how he had gotten so remarkably lucky. Then it was time to get up, wash, shave, and dress, and get moving.

"Oh my, look at you," Elspeth declared, eyes shining, when he walked into the kitchen.

"What?" He glanced down at his Sunday suit, hoping it wasn't stained or he hadn't put it on wrong.

Elspeth left the counter where she was buttering toast and came over to straighten his tie and brush her fingers through his carefully combed hair. He'd shaved and brushed his teeth to boot, even though he was about to eat. In fact, Elspeth stared at him as though she might like to gobble him up. He had to work not to scramble out of his clothes and do things on the kitchen table they would regret later.

"You, Mr. Athos Strong, musketeer, clean up very well," she said at last, pressing her hands to her pink, pink cheeks.

"Do I?" He took another look at himself. He had put extra effort into things. That hardly mattered. "You look like a fine and noble lady yourself today, wife of mine."

It was her turn to glance down at her dress—a pretty one made of blue material that contrasted perfectly with her porcelain complexion and dark hair. "Then we shall make the perfect picture of competent, responsible parents when we step into that courtroom today."

He was certain beyond doubt that she was right. It was the first time he was certain of anything, without any reservation, in as long as he could remember. They ate their breakfast while discussing the strategies they had planned with Solomon in meetings over the last week. Solomon was a true friend to come to their aid so selflessly, in spite of having his own business to run.

After breakfast and clean-up, they headed out, up Prairie Avenue and across Elizabeth Street to the town hall arm-in-arm. Maybe it was smug of him to strut so confidently, considering the order of the day, but with Elspeth on his arm, approving of his appearance, and with the morning they'd spent, how could he help but crow.

The town hall was already crowded by the time they arrived. All of the major players were there waiting, including the children.

"Papa! Papa!" they shouted from the far corner.

Mrs. Lyon stood with them on one side, wearing her stuffy grey suit and a peevish expression. Her guards lounged between her and the children, looking exhausted and put-out. The Bonneville clan, complete with sisters, Rex, and Cousin Rance, and an embarrassed-looking Bonnie stood nearby as well. None of them was fast enough to stop the Strong children when they saw their father and bolted.

"Papa, you look so handsome," Ivy declared breathlessly as the mass of children rushed across the room and into Athos and Elspeth's arms.

"You do, you do!" Millicent agreed, jumping up and down.

"You're almost too handsome to mess up with hugs," Heather said.

"Never," Athos declared, scooping as many of his children into his arms as he could for hugs and kisses.

"You look really pretty too, Lady Elspeth," Vernon said, staring at her with a boyish blush.

"Dear heavens, don't call me *Lady* anything." Elspeth threw her arms around Vernon as if he were her own son.

"That's what Miss Vivian and Miss Melinda say we have to call you," Geneva informed her.

Elspeth let go of Vernon to hug her. "Well, I think we all know what we can do with the opinions of Misses Vivian and Melinda."

Her simple comment was like opening the floodgates. "You'll never guess what Miss Melinda did yesterday," Lael began.

At the same time, Ivy blurted, "Miss Vivian smears

her face with buttermilk and mashed cucumbers at night!"

"Miss Bebe doesn't know how to tie her own shoes."

"Miss Melinda sat on a pinecone."

And on and on, all in a single rush of whispers and giggles.

Elspeth was roaring with laughter by the time Mrs. Lyon and her thugs marched over.

"Stop, stop, stop!" Mrs. Lyon scolded. "This is highly irregular and forbidden!"

It took all of Athos's powers of restraint to hold his tongue and not tell the shrewish woman exactly what he thought of her. Instead, he drew from the immense calm and beauty of the morning as it had unfolded so far and bowed like any good musketeer would. "Good morning, Mrs. Lyon."

"Wha—" Mrs. Lyon stared at him as though he had a frog on each shoulder, mouth hanging open. She shut it, shook her head, and huffed an impatient breath. "Good morning, Mr. Strong, Mrs. Strong. Get away from these children."

"These are my children," Athos said, surprised that he wasn't throttling the woman. "They only came over here to say good morning to their papa and their new mama."

"That's right, you *are* our new mama," Lael said.

"Wait, are we supposed to call you Mama or Lady Elspeth?" Millicent asked.

"Mama was Mama," Hubert said, frowning as though he'd just been presented with a mathematical problem.

"We discussed this before. You can call me just Elspeth," Elspeth laughed, ruffling Lael's hair.

"But shouldn't we—"

"Ugh, there he is." Before anything else could be

resolved, the Bonneville sisters left their spot at the side of the room and flounced over to join the Strongs. Or rather, Vivian, Melinda, and Bebe flounced, Honoria slunk.

"Lady Elspeth," Melinda said. "You don't have to stand by that odious man if you don't want to."

"Yes, we'll shelter you. We will always shelter people of quality and breeding," Vivian added.

"You're too good for him," Bebe finished. "We're too good for him too."

Elspeth's mouth dropped. She snuck a look at Athos. He just stood there grinning, eager to see how she would talk her way through this spectacle.

"Elspeth is nice," Thomas piped up. "I want to call her Mama. My other mama died before I could call her anything."

"Mrs. Lyon, aren't you supposed to be preventing these children from associating with their negligent father or bothering Lady Elspeth?" Vivian snapped.

Athos's annoyance was only outmatched by the surprise of Vivian sneering so viciously at a woman he thought was her ally.

"Yeah, do your job," Bebe added.

Evidently, the week hadn't been a pleasant one out at the Bonneville ranch. One covert glimpse at the children's knowing smirks and attempts not to laugh was proof of that.

"I would do my job if I had any sort of *support*," Mrs. Lyon snapped. "But no, I've been stuck with a bunch of preening, uptight, snobbish harpies who wouldn't know the meaning of discipline if it slapped them in the face, *which I would very much like to do*."

The children burst into snorts and giggles. Athos had a hard time keeping his own reaction in check. Elspeth covered her mouth with one gloved hand and turned partially away. It only got worse from there.

"Well, if *someone* wasn't such a sour old hypocrite, things would have gone much better," Melinda bit out.

"Me, a hypocrite?" Mrs. Lyon pressed a hand to her chest and gawped.

"You, madam, are the biggest hypocrite that has ever walked this earth," Vivian said, drawing herself up to her full height and staring down her nose at the woman. "You give yourself airs and pretend to be everyone's friend, then the moment it works to your advantage, you go running to papa in an attempt to stab them in the back. Every fruitful idea we have had for dealing with these wretched children you have attempted to steal and pass off as your own, and every time the winds were blowing against you, you attempted to throw us to the wolves instead of facing responsibility yourself."

"I never did any such thing," Mrs. Lyon bellowed.

Athos exchanged a glance with Elspeth, who looked every bit as much like she wanted to step back and let the hens peck each other to death as he did.

"You are a terrible manager of people." Melinda took up the cause as Vivian panted to catch her breath through her anger. "You can't even manage your own team, instead letting them run amok on our ranch." She threw out a hand to the four guards—who looked as though they would rather be anywhere else in the world.

"They all hate you, you know," Bebe added.

"They do not." Mrs. Lyon stomped her foot. "They respect me."

"Ha!" Melinda snorted. "They think you're a loud, shrill, incompetent, charlatan... charlataness?"

Mrs. Lyon yelped wordlessly in offense, looking from the Bonneville sisters to her toughs and back.

She was in the process of gathering her thoughts

when Solomon strode up to join their group. "The judge is on his way over from the hotel," he announced. When everyone around him failed to react, he blinked and twisted to study the variety of outraged and indignant expressions. "Did I miss something?"

Athos couldn't hold his laughter in for another moment. "We'll tell you later." He slapped Solomon on the back, shaking his head. "Children, go with Mrs. Lyon for now and behave."

"But Papa," they all began to protest at once.

"No, no, it's all right." He recovered from his laughter and the ridiculousness of the situation. "Elspeth and I will be right there in the courtroom with you. This will be quick, and then we can all go home and have a picnic lunch in the backyard."

"Yay!"

Led by Hubert, Ivy, and Heather, the children returned to their former spot on the other side of the room, the younger ones skipping and jumping as if nothing was wrong. Mrs. Lyon was red-faced and shaking as she walked back to stand with them. She didn't look at either her guards or the Bonneville sisters. For their part, the Bonneville sisters didn't seem to know whether to preen or pout. They sniffed and huffed and marched back across the room to their father.

All except for Honoria, who hung back.

"I think your plan to give my sisters reasons to get rid of the children as quickly as possible was a success, Mr. Templesmith," she said, cheeks pink and eyes bright as though she had been laughing too. It was the first time in a long time that Athos didn't think she looked sickly and defeated.

"Thank you, Miss Honoria." Solomon reached for her hand to shake it, and Honoria went pinker.

Then she fell into a coughing fit. With a quick nod, she turned and ran to join her family.

"I knew Miss Honoria would come through for us." Solomon smiled.

"The two of you seem to get along well," Elspeth said, grinning, her eyes sparkling.

For a moment, Solomon looked confused. "My dealings with the Bonnevilles have never been pleasant, but Honoria doesn't seem to take after her family."

Elspeth continued to grin. The gears in Athos's mind turned slowly, but if he wasn't mistaken, his lovely wife was making a romantic suggestion about Honoria Bonneville to Solomon.

There wasn't time to consider more. The town hall doors were flung open, and a grim, older man in an expensive suit walked into the room, Howard Haskell on one side, Theophilus Gunn on the other.

Chapter Thirteen

If Elspeth was taken aback by the sudden confrontation between Mrs. Lyon and the Bonneville sisters in the lobby of the town hall, it was nothing to the scene that unfolded in the courtroom. She couldn't have witnessed a more astounding show if Athos had bought the entire family tickets to the circus.

"This should be over quickly," Solomon advised them as they made their way into the main chamber of the town hall. It served as a courtroom sometimes and as a meeting place for the town council and other events the rest of the time. "All we need to do is present your side of the story, Athos, and I'm certain the judge will see things our way."

They passed through the doorway in time to see the Bonneville sisters rushing down one of the side aisles. Rex and Bonnie Horner, along with Cousin Rance, followed several feet behind, Rex and Rance wearing irritated scowls. Howard had escorted Judge Andrew Moss up to the large desk that formed the focal point of the room, and the two men stood conferring. That didn't stop Vivian and

Melinda from clearing their throats and fanning themselves and generally doing everything it took to draw the judge's attention. When the grim, older man finally did notice their antics, he narrowed his eyes and frowned at them. Melinda batted her eyelashes and waved, as if trying to catch the attention of an eligible bachelor at a summer dance. Judge Moss shook his head and turned back to Howard.

"I'm growing more confident in our case all the time," Athos murmured to Elspeth, grinning from ear to ear.

"How can they possibly think behavior like that will help their case in any way?" Elspeth giggled in return.

"I'm not sure it's the case that they're trying to get his help with," Athos replied.

"You know, I think you're right." Even though the thought was as repugnant as it was absurd.

Then again, Elspeth thought as Solomon led them to the first row of chairs on the opposite side from the Bonnevilles, Melinda Bonneville was exactly the sort who would marry a much older man for wealth or position.

She was spared having to think about or visualize that outcome any more than she already had as Mrs. Lyon led the Strong children into the room and down the center aisle. Elspeth's heart went out to Athos as he twisted in his chair, holding his breath as he watched his brood march in. Someone had gotten the idea to line them up in order from youngest to oldest, and judging by the pleased, almost smug looks on all of their faces, it wasn't Mrs. Lyon. Mrs. Lyon looked as fussy and put-out as ever, while every one of the Strong children wore cheerful smiles and walked sedately. In fact, if Elspeth wasn't mistaken, they had all dressed in their Sunday best and were scrubbed, combed, and polished to a shine. The four guards slumped in after them and took up positions at the back of the room.

As the children reached the section of seats in the front center of the room and filed quietly in, waiting, checking with each other, and sitting in unison, Elspeth couldn't contain her smile of pride. Not only did Athos's children—her children by extension—look like perfect angels, they had clearly plotted and rehearsed how they would handle the hearing. Elspeth snuck a careful look all the way across the room to Honoria and found her smiling with satisfaction at the children's display as well.

Judge Moss glanced up from his conversation with Howard behind the desk and frowned at the Strong children. "Is this it?" he asked, not knowing who to single out with his dark frown.

Mrs. Lyon stepped forward. She cleared her throat with a tight cough, then tilted her chin up. "I am Mrs. Margaret Lyon, representative from the Society for Prevention of Cruelty to Children, yes."

Judge Moss shook his head. "No, that's not what I mean. Are those the wild, irreverent, out-of-control children that have been taken from their father?" He gestured toward the row where the Strong children sat.

Each one of the Strong children sat straighter, hands folded in their laps, sweet smiles on their cherubic faces. Even Thomas managed to play along. Elspeth reached for Athos's hand with one of hers, covering her mouth to keep from laughing with the other.

"Yes, they are, but—" Mrs. Lyon paused. Her frown of frustration resolved into a smug grin. "They are, your honor, and as you can see, even a week away from their negligent father has done them a world of good. Imagine what changes could be wrought if they were given new homes entirely."

The older Strong children lost their smiles as they realized the tactic Mrs. Lyon was using. By Elspeth's side, Athos tensed. She squeezed his hand to reassure him.

"Wait this out," Solomon said on Athos's other side, reflecting Elspeth's thoughts.

"And you should see the state their home is in," Mrs. Lyon argued on. "Why, it's a perfect sty."

"No it isn't."

The room full of people who had come to watch the hearing turned as Pete Evans stood.

"Who are you?" Judge Moss asked.

"Peter Evans. I live next door to the Strong family, and I can assure you that their home is in perfect order," Pete said with every ounce of his considerable authority.

"Pete is one of the town's preeminent citizens," Howard told Judge Moss from his seat behind the desk.

"Is that so?" Judge Moss asked in response to both Howard and Pete. Mrs. Lyon's face pinched in fury as the Judge Moss nodded and said, "Go on."

"That house has been in perfect shape ever since Elspeth arrived and married Athos Strong," Pete said. "She'd got the whole thing in tip-top shape. The garden looks nice too."

"Yes, I agree." Josephine stood by Pete's side. "I'm Josephine Evans, by the way, your honor. Pete's wife. And I must say that ever since Elspeth and Athos got married, everything has been harmonious and tidy next door."

"But she only arrived and married him a week ago," Mrs. Lyon protested, throwing out her hands.

"Yes, and even a week of Elspeth being here has done a world of good," Josephine drawled, crossing her arms. "Imagine how lovely that home would be with a happy family in it."

The courtroom burst into chuckles and a spattering of

applause as Mrs. Lyon's words were turned back on her. Judge Moss had to wave his arms and call out, "Quiet, quiet!" Elspeth was sure that if he had a gavel, he would have banged it on the desk.

Athos leaned close to Elspeth and whispered. "Remind me to thank Josephine later." His smile was back, and once more Elspeth was confident in the direction of the hearing.

"The Society for Prevention of Cruelty to Children was assured in explicit language that the behavior of these children and their living situation was dire indeed," Mrs. Lyon went on, her voice shrill. "The court in Cheyenne followed the report that was given—a most explicit report that detailed outrageous behavior, disregard of the feelings of others, and disrespect toward neighbors, none of which was checked by the unfit person of Mr. Strong— and made their determination about the welfare of these children."

"Who filed the original report?" Judge Moss asked, unswayed by Mrs. Lyon's burst of emotion.

"They did." Mrs. Lyon threw out a hand toward the Bonnevilles.

Everyone in the room leaned forward, straining to see what Rex or his daughters would say. Rex sat stiff in his chair, arms crossed, staring straight forward. Bonnie looked mortified to be sitting there with them. Vivian, Melinda, and Bebe fussed with their dresses, plumped their hairstyles, and looked everywhere but at the judge or the spectators. Honoria shrank back in her chair, hand covering her mouth.

"Tell them!" Mrs. Lyon demanded.

"What is there to tell?" Vivian asked, batting her eyelashes and looking as innocent as she could.

"But—" Mrs. Lyon sputtered.

"*You* were the one who made us take them out to our ranch," Bebe sniffed. It was a shock to see her speaking for her entire family, but since the rest of them kept their mouths shut… "*We* never wanted them out there to begin with. We just wanted them to stop being such awful devils. And Vivian wanted revenge because her lilac dress was ruined."

"Bebe, be quiet," Rex growled under his breath.

"I'm just telling the truth," she said, then crossed her arms and slumped in a huff.

Judge Moss dragged his irritated stare back to Mrs. Lyon. "Do you have anything else you want to say?" He sounded bored and on the verge of giving someone a telling-off.

"N-no, your honor." Mrs. Lyon stepped back to her seat and plunked down, shoulders sagging.

Judge Moss turned to Solomon, Athos, and Elspeth. "Do you lot want to say something?"

Solomon stood. "You know, I had quite the defense planned. Testimonials, statistics, reference to the law. But after all that?" He nodded to the Bonneville's side of the room. "No, I think we can—"

"Yes." Athos cut Solomon off. "Yes, I would like to say something."

Elspeth's heart trembled with excitement as Athos stood, tugged the hem of his jacket, and straightened his tie. He took a few steps forward and turned to face the room. Solomon sat.

"I've been a father since I was nineteen years old," Athos said, addressing the people of Haskell more than Judge Moss. "That's far too young for anyone to start building a family, but it's what happened, and I wouldn't change it for anything."

He broke into a smile, focusing all of his attention on

his children. "You lot mean the world to me," he said, his voice thick with emotion. "Every one of you has been a blessing in my life. I'm not too proud to admit that I cried tears of joy when every one of you came into this world. I've changed your diapers, fed you, dressed you, forced you to brush your teeth when you didn't want to, tickled your bellies until you snorted."

The children—and several others in the room—laughed. Elspeth's eyes stung and her throat closed up. She pressed a hand to her pounding heart, more glad for the ring she wore telling the world she was this man's wife than for anything she'd ever known.

"We've had good times—like that Christmas your grandpa sent us sleds from Connecticut without realizing there aren't any hills nearby, so we made a train and dragged them through the streets instead."

"I remember that," Hubert spoke up, eyes bright with nostalgia. "You were so tired from playing reindeer at the end of the day that you fell asleep on the sofa, and we painted your face to look like Santa Claus."

The older children giggled at the memories, while the younger ones—who Elspeth guessed hadn't been born yet or were too young—looked on in wonder.

"We've been through bad times too," Athos continued. "It was hard losing your mother, harder than you'll ever know."

Ivy and Heather nodded, tears coming to their eyes. They hugged each other, while the older boys looked solemn.

"I loved her," Athos said quietly. "I did, even though we were both so busy and caught up in life to show it the way we should have. I wasn't a very good husband then, and I wasn't the best father I could have been."

"No!"

"No, Papa, you're the best."

"You're a wonderful father."

The children's protests brought tears to more than a few of the spectators.

"No." Athos held up his hand to stop them and shook his head. "I wasn't everything I could have been. But I promise you all that I'll be much better now. And now I have help. Mrs. and Mrs. Evans are right. Elspeth is a wonderful, remarkable woman." He stepped over to her, reaching for her hand. Elspeth shot to her feet, grasping his offered hand with both of hers. Athos gazed into her eyes and said, "I love her, and I promise you," he turned back to the children, "that our lives will all be so much better now that she's here with us."

"I love Elspeth too!" Thomas shouted. He leapt from his seat on the aisle and ran across the room to throw himself at Elspeth's legs. Several of the spectators laughed at his burst of affection.

Elspeth's heart felt as though it might break. She lifted Thomas and embraced him tightly. "I love you too, Thomas, and I always will."

"I'm going to call you Mama," he announced, then flopped his head to her shoulder, hugging her neck.

Elspeth peeked at Athos to see how he felt about that declaration. Her heart broke in earnest at the wide smile he wore and the bright glassy sheen to his eyes as he teetered near the edge of tears. He turned to Judge Moss and spread his arms wide, shrugging.

"You see, your honor. I may not be perfect, but without my children and my wife, I'm nothing at all. The house might not always stay clean. The children may stumble or act out from time to time. We might not be able to keep quiet when we all get excited. But these children are my life, my heart. And I…well, I'd like to think that I'm important to them as well."

"You are!"

"I love you, Papa."

"We should to home. We should all go home with Papa."

The children's statements were met by mutterings and outright calls of, "They should," by the people watching the hearing.

"Papa is my hero," Millicent exclaimed just as everyone else was quieting.

Athos laughed. "I'm not a hero, I'm just a father who loves his children."

"That's the best kind of hero of all," Elspeth said so that only he—and Thomas—could hear her. She reached for his hand with her free one and held it. "You're my hero, my musketeer."

Beaming with affection, Athos lifted her hand to his lips and kissed it. He turned back to Judge Moss. "Sir, I'd like to take my family home now. What do you say?"

The spectators in the courtroom hushed, leaning forward in their chairs expectantly. Across the front of the room, the Bonneville sisters looked on with wary indecision…all except Honoria, who was wiping tears from her eyes. Mrs. Lyon stood with her back stiff, her fists clenched at her sides, and her jaw so tight she was likely to end up with a headache.

"Well, Andrew? That is, Judge Moss." Howard spoke up from his seat behind the judge. "Do you need some time to deliberate?"

"No." Judge Moss's statement was definitive. "I've made my decision."

Chapter Fourteen

The courtroom hushed. Athos's heart beat so hard against his ribs that he could feel the reverberations through his entire body. His senses were alive, every nerve tingling since his speech. He was probably some new, ridiculous kind of fool for pouring out his emotions to his children and in public. Heroes were supposed to put on a brave front and never let the world see the tenderness underneath the armor.

But no, as he sent a glance to Elspeth—his lady and his strength—who looked so perfect and so right with Thomas cuddled in her arms, he knew that true heroes were the ones who were open enough to experience all of those emotions and to let the world see it as well. Love was never a bad idea.

Judge Moss cleared his throat and turned to Mrs. Lyon. "The Society for Prevention of Cruelty to Children is a noble cause with an important purpose."

Athos's certainty withered in his chest. He tightened his grip on Elspeth's hand.

Mrs. Lyon preened. "We like to think we're doing

vital work to protect the young people of America."

"Well, you're not," the judge barked. "Not here, at least."

Athos held his breath. He and Elspeth exchanged a quick, hopeful look. The children sat forward in their seats, confused and bristling with anticipation.

"I...I beg your pardon?" Mrs. Lyon sputtered.

Judge Moss shifted in his seat as though winding up for a pitch. "How dare you disrupt the lives of good, working folk under the guise of a charitable cause?"

His accusation was hurled with enough force to make the spectators gasp...and for Athos to release the breath he'd been holding. They'd won.

"I...I don't know what you mean." Mrs. Lyon's eyes were wide, and she searched madly around for someone to support her. She found nothing. The four men serving as her guards whispered to each other, then slipped out the back of the room.

"There is nothing wrong with this family," Judge Moss went on. "Trust me, Mrs. Lyon. I've seen disturbed children and young people whose past abuse led them to a sad life of crime. These children are no more in danger of becoming a menace to society than a tree frog."

Ripples of approval and a few calls of, "That's right," filled the room.

"Mr. Strong is a fine example of a father, and I order his children returned to him at once," Judge Moss went on.

Cheers and applause broke out from every corner of the room. Relief hit Athos so hard that he sagged, swaying close to Elspeth. The children jumped up from their seats and started to run to him as he held his hands out.

"Hold on, hold on!" Judge Moss shouted as the courtroom began to slip out of control.

"QUIET!" Howard boomed, standing and holding out his arms.

In an instant, everyone in the courtroom froze. Judge Moss flinched. He twisted to face Howard. "I should take you with me on my circuit."

"I'd be glad for the adventure," Howard laughed.

Judge Moss nodded to him, then turned to address Mrs. Lyon once more. "If you are so all-fired concerned with the welfare of young people, then I suggest you turn your attention to areas where children really could use an advocate."

"But…but I…I do," Mrs. Lyon whined.

"There are factories in this country where children are worked from dawn until dusk in terrible conditions," Judge Moss roared, utterly unsympathetic to her protest. "They work with dangerous machinery, losing limbs and even their lives. There are slums where children are starving, where they are abandoned to the depravities of evil men and women. There are mines and logging camps where they are treated no better than animals. Those are the places you should be turning your efforts."

"But," Mrs. Lyon continued to protest with barely enough energy to hold her head up. "But those places are *dirty*. They're dangerous."

"That is exactly my point," Judge Moss insisted.

"I…I don't want to go to *those* places," Mrs. Lyon finished, her voice fading away.

"Then get out of my sight, woman." He thrust a finger at the door. "You are no more a champion of the downtrodden than you are a sultan in Egypt."

Mrs. Lyon cowered, gathering her skirts and rushing to leave the room. Across from where Athos stood, watching the whole thing in wonder, the Bonneville sisters sniggered and gloated.

"And you!" Judge Moss turned his ferocious glare on them.

Vivian, Melinda, and Bebe stopped mid-snicker, eyes going round. Rex rolled his eyes and crossed his arms. Beside him, Bonnie pursed her lips and leaned away, as if trying to separate herself from the family. Cousin Rance blinked as if he had no clue what was going on. Honoria shrunk in the corner.

"You," Judge Moss went on, "should know better than to drag good people through this sort of trauma simply to seek revenge for some imagined slight."

"It wasn't imagined," Bebe blurted. "They ruined Vivian's lilac dress and my spring green one. That dress came all the way from Paris!"

"Actually, Wendy Montrose made it," Honoria mumbled, just loud enough for everyone to hear.

"Shut up, Honoria," Bebe snapped.

"Shut up, Bebe." Vivian smacked her sister on the arm.

"If I hear so much as a peep of any of your names mentioned in any legal documents that come my way from here on out," Judge Moss thundered over them. "I will immediately tear those documents to shreds and dismiss any suits or claims you bring before the court."

"What about marriage certificates?" Vivian squeaked, turning pale.

"Any man foolish enough to marry you deserves what he gets," the judge grumbled.

"Hey, wait a minute." Rance came out of his confused haze.

Before any of them could say anymore, Judge Moss stood and declared, "This case is closed. You all can go back to your father now."

Another round of applause and cheers followed as

the children resumed their rush out of their seats and across to where Athos and Elspeth stood. The crush of so many children coming at him all at once nearly knocked Athos off his feet, but he would have gladly suffered every bruise if it meant he could have his family with him always.

"I knew you could do it, Papa!"

"Papa, you're the best!"

"You're my hero!"

The outpouring of love from his children was almost more than Athos could take. He made a point to hug every single one of his kids, even Hubert, who under normal circumstances would have rather died than have his father hug him in public.

"I love you, I love you, I love you. I love every one of you," he said, sighing with relief.

"We love you too, Papa!"

"And we love you, Elspeth," Ivy shifted to hug Elspeth, who still held an excited Thomas in her arms.

"Me?" Elspeth laughed, her expression startled. "But you barely know me."

"You tried to rescue us when we were trapped at the Bonneville ranch," Lael insisted, edging his way through his siblings so he could stand close to her side.

"Yeah, and you look really pretty," Geneva added.

Elspeth laughed even harder. "Well, I promise I'll do my best to be worthy of all this love."

"Yay!"

"And Aunt Piper will love you too," Millicent added.

"Piper!" Athos slapped a hand to his head.

"What? What's wrong?" Elspeth asked.

Athos turned to her, laughing at himself. "Can you believe that with all the fuss and...and activity this week—" His face went hot at the memory of activity he wouldn't be telling the children about. "I forgot to telegraph Piper to tell her what was going on."

"You forgot to tell Aunt Piper we were taken away?" Heather asked, incredulous.

"It was a busy week," Athos defended himself. "And everything turned out for the best in the end."

"I can't wait to tell her everything," Vernon snorted. "She's gonna be so mad at you, Papa."

The threat struck real fear into him. Piper in a snit was fearsome indeed, and this would put her in the snittiest snit she'd ever had. "Maybe we could just wait to tell her until she gets back here in August."

The children nodded and giggled and approved of the idea.

"Congratulations, Athos." Solomon stepped into the family group, thumping Athos on the back.

"Solomon, thank you so much." Athos turned to shake his hand. "I'm not sure we could have won this without you."

"Nonsense." Solomon waved away the compliment. "As soon as the judge saw all of you together, anything I could have said was irrelevant."

"Still, if there's ever anything we can do to repay you," Elspeth said.

Solomon shook his head. "I wouldn't think of it." Before Athos could protest, Solomon nodded past their group. "I think someone else has something to say."

They turned to see Honoria approaching. She glanced over her shoulder to where her family was gathering their things to leave. "Thank you, Mr. Templesmith," she said, almost in a whisper, then stole the rest of the way into the group.

"Miss Honoria, Miss Honoria." The children crowded around her, giving her hugs.

Honoria blushed as if taken aback by the sudden outpouring of affection. "I just wanted to say that I'm happy things worked out for you." She opened her mouth to say more, but started coughing.

"Are you well, Miss Honoria?" Solomon asked.

"Miss Honoria is sick," Thomas told him. He shifted to say to Elspeth, "She coughs all the time and she has headaches."

"She lies down a lot," Neva added.

"She tries to," Lael went on. "The other Miss B's always yell at her to get up."

"Miss Bonnie told her to go to the doctor," Ivy finished.

"I will, I will," Honoria insisted.

"Honoria! Get over here! We're leaving," Vivian barked from the other side of the room.

Honoria sent a worried look over her shoulder, then said, "I'd better go."

She started to leave, but Elspeth stopped her with, "Wait."

Honoria paused, sending Elspeth a worried, regret-filled look.

"I hope you know that the Strong family are your friends," Elspeth rushed to say. "We'll always be your friends. Please call on us for help any time."

"Honoria!" Vivian bellowed.

"I will," Honoria whispered, then rushed off to join her family, coughing up a storm.

"I'm worried about her," Athos spoke his thought aloud.

"If ever a young woman needed an advocate, it's her," Solomon agreed.

Elspeth turned to him, a glittering light in her eyes. "Then why don't you do something about it?"

"Me?" Solomon shook his head and shrugged in confusion. "What can I do to help her?"

"I don't know." Elspeth glanced across the room to study Honoria as she rejoined her family and was jerked along to the door. "But be ready in case something presents itself."

They paused, watching until the Bonnevilles were gone. Then Athos shook away the unsettled feeling Honoria left him with and turned to his children, his family, with a broad smile. "Come on," he said. "It's time for all of us to go home. Just you wait until you see how clean the house is."

"And we're going to keep it that way, aren't we?" Elspeth asked as they headed out of the courtroom in a group.

"Yes, Elspeth," the children answered.

"Yes, Mama," Thomas said, even louder.

The children laughed, then the younger ones hopped and leaped and bounded on their way out of the courtroom.

"Still full of energy, even after a bout of the Bonnevilles," Elspeth joked.

"I don't think anything could drain the energy out of my children," Athos said, taking Elspeth's hand. "Out of *our* children."

"And that's why I love them," she smiled. She stopped long enough to lean over and kiss him. "That's why I love you."

Epilogue

The heat of late July was stifling, but it wasn't enough to stop the Strong family from coming out in full force to celebrate Thomas's fifth birthday.

"I'm five today," Thomas told Pete Evans, then ran across the shaded back lawn of the Strong house to tell Franklin and Corva Haskell and their baby, "I'm five today."

He rushed on, barging into the group that consisted of Elspeth, Katie Murphy, Emma Meyers, and Wendy Montrose and her brand new baby.

"Guess what?" he asked, hugging Elspeth around the waist.

"Are you five today?" Katie asked in her lilting Irish brogue.

Thomas stopped, jaw dropping. "How did you know?"

"I might have heard it from someone," Katie teased.

"I'm gonna go tell someone else," Thomas announced and ran off.

The adults were left to laugh. Elspeth's heart felt too

big for her chest as she watched him. It did every time she watched any of the children play. "I think he's made his way through all the women. He'll start bothering your husbands next."

"Not ours," Emma said.

Katie hummed in agreement, then added, "Aiden and Dean were called off to the Cheyenne camp earlier. There's been a bit of fuss between the Cheyenne and the soldiers."

"But if anyone can smooth things over, it's Dean and Aiden."

Elspeth didn't know much about the situation with the Indians who lived nearby. All she knew was that Aiden Murphy and Dr. Dean Meyers were liaisons between the tribe and the government, and they were called away more often than not. It was a good thing Haskell had two doctors, otherwise they'd be left in a lurch when Dr. Meyers was away on other work.

"I'll bet you'll have even more children running around this yard before too long," Emma shifted the conversation, looking across the running, climbing, giggling mass of children to find her own kids.

"We've only been married for about eight weeks." Elspeth grinned, glancing across the lawn to where Athos was standing with Solomon and all three Montrose brothers. From the gestures they were using, they were discussing last week's baseball game, in which Athos had hit a homerun for the Eastside Eagles. The fact that he was finally able to take the time to play baseball was just another way that their lives had improved since the new station assistant, Roman Danville, had moved to town.

"Eight weeks was more than enough for me," Katie laughed.

"It's more than enough for plenty of women," Emma agreed with a wink.

Elspeth tilted her head to the side in thought. "I don't know what the future will bring. I was involved with a man for almost a year, and not once was there a hint of a baby." She'd been open with her new friends about her past, figuring they all knew the pitfalls that women could fall into.

"Do you think you'd be happy if you didn't have any of your own?" Wendy ventured to ask, snuggling her own baby.

Elspeth's smile returned as she watched Lael gather a group of younger boys together to climb trees as part of whatever game they were playing. Off in another corner of the yard, Ivy and Heather were having what appeared to be a dignified discussion with Freddy Chance, Noah Kline, and a few of the other boys that were just a tad too old for them. Meanwhile, Geneva and Millicent were helping Muriel Chance and some of her friends with babies that various party guests had handed over to them so they could have grown-up conversations. Vernon and Hubert seemed to be discussing baseball techniques with some of the other older boys. And Thomas was still tearing around, telling everyone he was five years old.

"I think I would," Elspeth concluded. "We're so blessed with a loving family already."

Across the yard, Athos glanced up and caught her eye. Elspeth thought back to their early morning shenanigans, the way they'd tried hard to keep silent and not wake the children. He must have been thinking the same thing. His face flushed, and he left his friends to stride over to join her, like a conquering hero returning home.

"But I wouldn't say no to more," Elspeth added for her friends before he reached her.

"More what?" Athos asked, slipping an arm around her waist and kissing her cheek.

At that moment, Elspeth spotted Honoria hurrying down the street. She looked pale and hugged herself as if she was cold, even though the sun was blazing above them. One quick glimpse and Elspeth could see she was crying.

"More…" Her answer to Athos's question faded as she broke away and rushed through the yard.

She met Honoria a few feet past the edge of the Strong property.

"Honoria, what's wrong?" she called, getting close enough to touch Honoria's arm.

Honoria stumbled, then spun toward Elspeth, hurling herself against her for a hug. Alarmed, Elspeth embraced her tightly. Honoria was trembling.

"What's wrong?" Elspeth repeated.

Honoria tugged away. She turned this way and that, looking confused, lost. She started forward, then hung back as if she didn't know what do to. Her erratic behavior was cut short by a bout of wracking coughs that nearly doubled her over. She started crying all over again.

"Oh dear." Elspeth rushed to hug her again. "Please, please tell me what's wrong, Honoria."

"I…I…" Honoria hid her face against Elspeth's shoulder, then whispered, "I'm dying."

Panic struck Elspeth's heart. "What? No, there must be some mistake."

"Elspeth?"

When Elspeth twisted to answer Athos's questioning call, Honoria broke out of her arms and started running down Prairie Avenue.

"Miss Honoria?" Solomon — who had come to

investigate along with Athos—called out in his deep baritone.

The two men sped out into the street. Athos caught Elspeth in his arms.

"What's wrong? You look upset." He hugged her.

"Honoria...Honoria just told me she was dying," Elspeth said, barely above a whisper.

Solomon frowned, glancing between Athos and Elspeth and Honoria's retreating back. "I'll go after her," he said, then jogged on to catch up with her.

For a moment, Elspeth's spirits lifted. For the past six weeks she'd been trying to orchestrate another meeting between Solomon and Honoria. But after what Honoria had just whispered, what could possibly come of it now?

"Come back to the party," Athos encouraged her in a tender voice. "Solomon will get to the bottom of it. I'm sure things aren't as bad as all that."

Heart still aching with worry, Elspeth tried to put on a smile. "I'm sure you're right."

"I'm always right." Athos smiled, kissing her tenderly right there in the street. "Except when you're right. Which is most of the time," he added with a laugh.

She tried to laugh along with him, but ended up hugging him for all she was worth. "I don't know what I'd do without you, Athos."

"Lucky for you, you don't have to find out." He squeezed her tight. "And I'm sure whatever it is can't be as bad as all that."

"No." Elspeth inched back so that she could look into her husband's eyes, cradling the sides of his face with her hands. "And if there is something wrong, we'll be there to help her."

"We will," Athos agreed. He stole one more kiss, then

smiled. "I should have listened to advice and sent away for you, my lady love, so much sooner than I did."

"I'm here now," she reassured him, happiness filling her heart once more. "And that's all that matters."

Wait, what? What just happened to Honoria? Is she really dying? And how could Solomon possibly help something so dire? You'll just have to come back for more in a few weeks when *His Forbidden Bride* comes out! Honoria and Solomon had much, much more story to be told!

About the Author

I hope you have enjoyed *His Remarkable Bride*. If you'd like to be the first to learn about when new books in the series come out and more, please sign up for my newsletter here: http://eepurl.com/RQ-KX And remember, Read it, Review it, Share it! For a complete list of works by Merry Farmer with links, please visit http://wp.me/P5ttjb-14F.

Merry Farmer is an award-winning novelist who lives in suburban Philadelphia with her two cats, Butterfly and Torpedo. She has been writing since she was ten years old and realized one day that she didn't have to wait for the teacher to assign a creative writing project to write something. It was the best day of her life. She then went on to earn not one but two degrees in History so that she would always have something to write about. Her books have topped the Amazon and iBooks charts and have been named finalists in the prestigious RONE and Rom Com Reader's Crown awards.

You can email her at merryfarmer20@yahoo.com or follow her on Twitter @merryfarmer20.

Merry also has a blog, http://merryfarmer.net, and a Facebook page, www.facebook.com/merryfarmerauthor

Acknowledgements

I owe a huge debt of gratitude to my awesome beta-readers, Caroline Lee and Jolene Stewart, for their suggestions and advice. And a big, big thanks to my editors, Cissie Patterson and Jackson D'Lynne, for doing an outstanding job, as always, and for leaving hilarious comments throughout the manuscript. Also, a big round of applause for my marketing and promo mistress, Sara Benedict.

And a special thank you to the Pioneer Hearts group! Do you love Western Historical Romance? Wanna come play with us? Become a member at https://www.facebook.com/groups/pioneerhearts/

Other Series by Merry Farmer

The Noble Hearts Trilogy
(Medieval Romance)

Montana Romance
(Historical Western Romance – 1890s)

Hot on the Trail
(Oregon Trail Romance – 1860s)

**The Brides of Paradise Ranch –
Spicy and Sweet Versions**
(Wyoming Western Historical Romance – 1870s)

Willow: Bride of Pennsylvania
(Part of the American Mail-Order Brides series)

Second Chances
(contemporary romance)

The Advisor
(Part of The Fabulous Dalton Boys trilogy)

The Culpepper Cowboys
(Contemporary Western - written in partnership with
Kirsten Osbourne)

New Church Inspiration
(Historical Inspirational Romance – 1880s)

Grace's Moon
(Science Fiction)

42427480R00125